Back on Tuesday

Back on Tuesday is an extremely funny book, a litany of the hero's excesses with alcohol, drugs and women. Gilmour's prose is a surging tide of humour, erudition, slang and foul language. It seduces and fascinates. Ultimately, *Back on Tuesday* enriches the body of confessional literature. — MACLEAN'S

In *Back on Tuesday*, we are given ostentatious passages of meditation, polemic and remembrances of sins past — interspersed by bouts of vomiting. This kind of review might be considered a slap against a first novel. *Back on Tuesday*, though, provokes it. — TORONTO STAR

Back on Tuesday

DAVID GILMOUR

The Coach House Press Toronto

To Anne Mackenzie and to John Allen

Thanks to the people at Coach House
and especially to David Young

Published with the assistance of
the Canada Council and
the Ontario Arts Council

CANADIAN CATALOGUING IN
PUBLICATION DATA

Gilmour, David, 1949-
Back on Tuesday

ISBN: 0-88910-293-7
PS8563.I56B33
1986   C813'.54   C86-093760-1
PR9199.3.G55B33 1986

SECOND PRINTING

No, I didn't kidnap the child. You can't kidnap your own child. Well you could, I suppose, but I never would. No, that wasn't it. Nor was it as simple as I pretended at the time: that I simply took her to Jamaica without telling her mother.

Anyway to my credit I was cold sober when I did it. At the beginning.

Chapter One

It must have been the photograph that set things off, although I didn't know it at the time. I'd dropped around J.'s apartment to pick up my daughter's bicycle helmet. It was ten o'clock on a muggy September morning and the place was empty. I'd often been in the apartment since we split up. And while it was none of my business, sometimes, when I was there alone, I couldn't resist a little snoop around – a peek at the phone bill, the long distance calls, the notice board, the odd letter ... nothing creepy or lurky, just a casual look around. I mean I wasn't tearing back the sheets or anything.

By now she was living with a guy who looked like a Turkish terrorist. He was sort of interesting really, although I had a bone to pick with him and it had nothing to do with J. He got honked at a party once and threatened me. He had me backed right up against the kitchen fridge. I must have run that scenario through my mind a thousand times in the weeks that followed. It made me feel sick every time.

7

When I was in the apartment, I checked out his papers too.

Over a period of time, a generous period of time I have to admit, it became clear to me that I was less and less of an issue in her life. My books vanished, got lent or the child scribbled in them. My father's gold pocket-watch disappeared. It wasn't a question of her pushing me out of her life. I was just slipping away, a natural evolution. I was being shelved and I knew it.

We seldom talked; when we did it was about the child, about babysitters, sugar fits, about who was picking her up after daycare and so on and so on. But there was no time between us.

It was annoying, painful but temporary I thought. A year went by, then two years. And things only got more distant, more business-like. She'd 'gotten over' me, to say the least. In her apartment I found the reminders of my unimportance painful. To be blunt about it, that's why I stopped snooping around.

So this one hot day I'm scratching around looking for Franny's helmet. And I see a letter and a photograph on the kitchen table. No, I say to myself, leave it alone. I even congratulate myself for my strength of character.

But I couldn't resist a look, a tiny peek. It was a picture of a lovely apple yard. It must have been spring because the grass was still flattened and there were red knots of sprouts on the trees.

And there they were: Franny, J., the terrorist and J.'s father. They were looking at something with great interest, a house maybe, a willow branch, who knows. That's not the point. The point is that, corny as it sounds, it was the picture of a family. And I wasn't in it. And, to put it delicately, they didn't look any the worse for it.

I picked up the helmet, went back down the stairs and back to the film festival office. I said nothing to J. But now, looking back on the events of the next twenty-four hours, I think that must have been the start of it.

Yet when I think back on that summer, it wasn't as chilly between me and J. as it seemed at the time. Now, with a cooler head I remember moments of undenied intimacy, refrains of the old magic – an ease with each other that we shared like a mutual skin. She came into my office once and in front of everyone asked if she could borrow my toothbrush. She wanted to brush her teeth because the terrorist was flying in from Vancouver that afternoon. But that didn't matter. It seemed like such a trusting gesture, the closest we'd been in some time. It was, if nothing else, an admission of shared history and I was proud of her.

And then there was the time in the hallway of her apartment. We were both in a frantic hurry, I can't remember why, and J. was flying about, smoking a cigarette, washing the dishes, talking about firing the babysitter when suddenly, in the middle of it, she decided to change her shirt and she took it off without missing a beat. Or turning her back. It was the first time in three years she did that. It was as if we were so engrossed in the conversation that we forgot we weren't together anymore. Or perhaps she was in too much of a rush to remind me that we weren't.

And when I caught myself looking at her, trying to keep at eye level, I had, I confess, the sensation of looking over a very high building, the same way I used to feel when I slept on the couch of one of her boyfriends and at three o'clock in the morning I'd hear her slip quietly out of bed and tiptoe into my room. 'Are you awake?' she'd whisper and even in the dark she knew my eyes were open.

That afternoon in the hallway there was a glimmer of that, but in the next seconds I felt myself retreating as if through inverted binoculars.

Those isolated moments ... and others, barely audible refrains which, I sometimes suspect, only I heard.

One afternoon, I found myself walking behind her on a quiet street. It startled me. She didn't know I was there.

She seemed preoccupied, deeply absorbed in her own thoughts. I had the uncomfortable sensation of being about to interrupt a very private moment. I wanted to duck down a side street, to leave her to it when, abruptly, she turned around as if guided by intuition.

'I was just thinking about you,' she blurted out. I should have pressed the point. I should have looked right at her and asked. But I didn't.

What could she have been thinking? Was she wondering how long it had been since we were together? Was she wondering what it was we'd loved about each other? Or was she thinking that she didn't know what I was like anymore?

Anyway I didn't ask. But I've often wished I had.

And would it have made any difference? At some point we all think about everything, even the dead.

Perhaps I tried to hang onto J. too long. Too many visits, too many lingering phone calls ... twenty dollars here, thirty dollars there.... 'Say J., can you spot me a fin til Friday.... How's the health insurance?... I think I've got strep throat coming on.... Listen, I just popped in to see Franny, I should have called.... Just the pork chops, please, I'm in a bit of a rush.... Say J., do you think they'll mind if I come to the party too?'

No wonder she despised me near the end. You can't

run away from home if you keep popping in for dinner.

Indeed I find it difficult to understand how I could have been so naive to think that things could possibly go back to those other times before, when she had a boyfriend and I had a girlfriend and we hung around all night, saw the dawn rise a million times in a delicious conspiracy of friendship.

So it's true I suppose. When she stopped paying attention, I found it infuriating. To have her eyes flit away in the middle of a conversation, to have her reach for a phone; to have her ask me a question only to lose interest in the answer.

What stung was that it was unintentional, all the more painful because it wasn't meant to hurt. But it was an indifference that left you totally impotent, as if when in total exasperation you threw up your hands and shrieked 'You're not listening. You never listen. You never touch me anymore; you never....'

You find yourself braying like a goat with its head caught in the outhouse door.

And she looks at you with calculated bewilderment.

'What *are* you talking about?'

We all have ways of punishing people. J.'s was to forgive them. Mine was to disappear. Ten years ago, at the end of my first year in university, I stopped by her place one spring evening to find a note on the door.

'Please. No visitors until after the exams.' It was J.'s handwriting but her roommate's idea. She'd objected to my comings and goings. This was J.'s way of dealing with it. I found it mightily offensive and vanished into the record room of the Central Library for four days – as long as it took her to find me.

Then it was back to more sunrises, scrambled eggs, cigarettes and Leonard Cohen records.

I don't recount this story with any pride; its implications don't escape me. I say it straight for the record. I disappear when I'm hurt.

I realize now that she won't come after me anymore. I can wait in the record room until the century changes and she still won't come. Somewhere back there she stopped noticing if I didn't call, if a day or a week went by without us seeing each other. She doesn't notice if I leave without saying goodbye.

And it's odd that it bothers me after these many years. Perhaps I'm whining but it's hard sometimes to feel that invisible, as if she might reach right through me for an ashtray.

And this business about Jamaica, about taking the child with me. It was, I suppose, a way of upping the ante. God knows, it may have been years before she noticed if I'd gone by myself. But we're not in school anymore. That stuff doesn't work anymore. It's obscenely out of date.

Besides it'll never be the same between us again. And I suppose this is the last kick at the can before, in my own heart, I too let the whole thing go.

But back to the photograph. I was working for J. at the time, natch. She'd hired me to write the program book for that fall's film festival. The day of the photograph, that was the day the book came out. It looked terrific, gleaming black covers, the pages were in the right order, none of the advertisements was upside down. It was really all right and that was the most you could hope for. Besides I was thirty and I'd never published anything before. It was a big deal and perhaps I made a little too much of it.

We were in the office, right after a little celebration in the hotel bar downstairs. I was there. So was J., so were a dozen other people – fundraisers, secretaries, so and so from the Godard retrospective, the box-office manager, the patrons' committee, a couple of drivers, the hotel manager – everyone sitting around smoking cigarettes, drinking beer, chatting about the festival, the book, a bit of gossip, jokes, all that.

Outside it had turned into a filthy day: dark clouds, low and ugly. It looked like trouble. From where I was sitting it looked more like a winter's afternoon than five o'clock the first week of September. You could see cracks of lightning fire over the lake.

Then the rain started.

And then the phone rang. Amid all the chatter no one heard it, except J. There was a moment which even at the time struck me as odd. She was staring at me. The phone rang again and she kept staring, waiting, or so it seemed, for me to pick it up. It was like a command. She'd been drinking – we all had – and when she drinks her face becomes pale and the skin is drawn taut, almost translucent, over her high cheek bones. She looked deathly. And strangely angry as if some tape, some image unconnected to the room, was running through her memory and had settled on me the very moment the phone rang. I reached over, taking my eyes away from her and picked up the phone.

It was Taffy, Fran's babysitter. She was phoning from J.'s apartment. A fuse had blown; there was no power. The two of them were stuck in the kitchen, in the black. And I remember thinking: Then change the fuse. But she couldn't; she'd never learned how. I was a little drunk and I said, rather testily, 'You're nineteen years old and you don't know how to change a fuse?' I knew what she wanted. She wanted someone to race across town in the rain and do it for her. And I found that irritating. So I told her, in some detail, where the fuse box was and how to change the fuse.

'How will I find the fuse box?' she queried. 'It's too dark.'

'Take a candle and light it.'

'What will I do with Franny while I'm in the basement changing the fuse?'

'Take her with you,' I said evenly, perhaps too evenly because I saw J. shoot me a frown across the room. She hadn't picked up the gist of the conversation but she recognized the tone. I put the phone down.

J. asked, loudly, from the other side of the room, what the call was about. I explained.

She paused and I knew what would happen next.

Affecting bewilderment, she snapped, 'Why don't you get into a taxi and go do it?'

She didn't raise her voice but the annoyance was picked up around the room and some of the conversations fell silent.

'Because I told her how to do it.'

Then I added a lie. 'I told her to call back if she can't do it.'

'But why don't you just go and do it?'

'It's your apartment,' I retorted. But it came out wrong. It sounded truculent, petty and I had a sudden sinking feeling that the room had turned against me. By now all but a few people were listening. They were staring at their drinks or lighting cigarettes or pretending to be absorbed by something else but they were listening and it made my heart thump with self-consciousness.

And then I sank further into the quicksand.

'She's nineteen years old! I think it's outrageous that

a nineteen year old who's entrusted with our child can't change a fuse.'

It struck entirely the wrong note. I might as well have launched into a tirade about 'young people today.' Coming from a man who didn't learn to cook until he was twenty-eight ... it sounded ridiculous, even to me. The words tumbled weakly from my mouth and plopped straight onto the floor.

J. said nothing, savouring the hole I'd dug for myself.

The room chilled another ten degrees. I swear I heard someone say, in a voice brimming with contempt, 'Why doesn't he just go?'

'Why don't you just go?' J. repeated. Her face was pinched. Even her eyes seemed smaller.

'She'll call if she can't do it.' My voice went up a register. I sounded like a frightened adolescent. I had completely lost control of the situation. And had made myself look like a boor in the process.

'If there's a problem,' I started in ... but she interrupted me.

'Just go.'

And then it snapped.

'I don't want to!' I screamed and my voice broke again. I slammed my hand on the desk, knocking beer bottles into the air and upsetting an ashtray. I came around the side of my desk. J. retreated behind hers.

The office emptied; they scattered like cockroaches; they didn't put down their bottles or pick up their purses or butt their cigarettes; they just beat it. No one was smiling. In a minute J. and I were the only ones left. And a secretary; she was too terrified to move, sat at her typewriter, stony faced, pecking mechanically at the keys. A head popped around the corner, hissed, crooked a finger. The girl jumped to her feet and slipped out of the room.

'Gene,' she said conciliatorily. I slammed the desk again.

'Don't use that night-nurse tone on me.'

'Gene, I was trying to....'

'You were meddling, you cunt. You were sticking your nose where it didn't belong.'

'I was....'

'You were being a cunt, that's what you were doing. I had it under control. You messed it up. So take charge; go home and change the fuse.'

Then I remembered she was afraid of electricity. In those seconds, while the crack from my hand on the desk still echoed, I remembered that I had never seen her change a plug or a fuse in all the years I'd known her. That made me cold and bloodthirsty. 'She can't change the fuse,' I yelled. 'You'll have to go home and help her. You'll have to do it yourself. You'll have to stumble around in the basement in the dark or the two of them will sit there all night. You're the boss; you're in charge.'

I took another step towards her.

'I don't have time,' she said, a flutter in her voice. She was on the run. 'I have too much to do here. I'm behind; everything starts in a week; I can't leave.'

She must have felt herself slipping because she changed beats. She adopted a cool, professional tone but there was a tremor; it was such a transparent attempt at diplomacy I had to laugh. She didn't want to change that fuse and it was dawning on her that she might have overplayed her hand.

But I was hot, too angry to defer. I wanted to stay mad for a while.

She paused for a second, looked down, then made a curious gesture with both hands, as if she were pushing down the lid on a garbage can. Now the voice was even more rational and I knew she was panicking. I confess, not without a little disgust, I wanted to run her to tears.

'I have a board meeting at six. I haven't booked one of the Casavettes films. He's calling here in half an hour....'

She rhymed off a list. 'I can't leave.'

'Fuck them.'

'I can't, Gene.'

I was getting closer to her.

'And don't speak to me as if I'm crazy.' I was very close now and I said, in a whisper, 'Just go.'

She looked at me and I could see she was frightened.

'Get out of here,' she said.

'No, you go.'

I thought she'd fire me on the spot. But she didn't.

'The book is a mess,' she said quietly. 'It's full of mistakes. I should have got somebody else.'

That staggered me.

'You drink too much. You shouldn't have proofed it when you were drunk. I shouldn't have hired someone who couldn't keep it together the last three days.'

'I wasn't drunk. What are you talking about?'

'You were drinking that stupid overproof when you were proofing the art boards. Peg told me.'

I sat down.

'Now this is my office. Get out,' she said. I looked up. I opened my mouth; I wanted to tell her I hated her, how glad I was I'd left her, fucked around on her. But I heard the words as I thought them; they sounded so petty, so wounded, I let them crash around inside my skull until they came to a halt. Besides, there's leaving and there's leaving. I may have left but she didn't come back.

We sat there, hearts beating, like two trapped animals, neither looking at the other while outside the rain poured and the lightning cracked, and we heard nothing of it through the thick glass of the window panes. For the first time in three years I had a craving for a cigarette. They were on her desk.

Chapter Two

'I should have got someone else.' That rang in my ear like I'd been slapped with a twenty-pound boxing glove.

Was she talking about a husband or an editor? Probably both.

When I got out of the elevator it was pouring rain. I stormed through the revolving doors, snapping an elderly lady into the lobby behind me. The streetlights were on; cars inched forward, their fog lights and headlights glistening. Within half a block my glasses streamed with water and I sprinted along the street. I slowed to a jog, then a walk, and in the rain I could feel the momentum of my anger slipping away. I began to think that maybe it was my fault, that maybe J. had been exaggerating, that maybe the book wasn't really a mess and that I'd flown off the handle for nothing. I thought with each step that I was the guilty one, I'd escalated it, she'd been under a lot of strain and I'd pushed her over the top and now she'd have to fire me. Or maybe she wouldn't hire me next year. What would I do? How would I earn my living?

I worked myself into a real state of panic and I started to think that it was imperative to go back and see her, to make up, to get through this thing. If only for the sake of the child. We couldn't have these terrible fights. I'd have to stop seeing the child, all because of a stupid, boozy quarrel about a couple of spelling mistakes in a book that would be outdated ten days after the festival was over.

But I shouldn't have banged the desk like that. Or threatened her. What if she fired me? What about next year?

My mind was racing so fast, so out of control that I wasn't watching where I was going and I stepped out in front of a car. It honked; the honk was followed by a head popping out the window. 'You moron! Look where you're going.'

It startled me so much my feet slipped from under me and I crashed onto the pavement, into a puddle in the gutter. I was soaked; my glasses flew off and landed beside me with a plop; one of the lenses popped out and lay like a turtle on the pavement. I was too rattled to do anything but scoop it up and sweep back along the street, my shoes squelching, my hair hanging in idiot strings across my forehead.

What if she had already left? I should have taken a cab, I should have gone back and changed the fuse, I shouldn't have exploited her fear of electricity. I should have proofed the galleys more thoroughly. I should have checked the credits myself. I shouldn't have left it to Rachel. I bet she made a million mistakes. I bet that was what J. was talking about.

What if she was gone? There was a hundred yards between me and the office and I broke into a sweaty run. What if she wasn't alone? What if the secretaries had come back? How could we talk in front of the secretaries?

And looking at my reflection in the elevator overhead mirror, I wondered how I had ever become so weak and frightened. And how long had it been going on.

J. wasn't alone. In her bright, white, light-swept office she talked on the telephone. Beside her the obedient troll, Peg, typed. She frowned when I came in. She was J.'s first lieutenant, privy to the secrets, the gossip and the rumours. She fancied herself a protective wall between J. and an uncivilized world of people wanting things. We despised each other. Tonight, she typed happily, contented there was no one but the two of them, just her and J., alone and working hard.

'It's been taken care of,' she said frostily. 'The power is back on.'

'Oh, good,' I said, relieved.

She resumed her typing dismissively. I remained standing in front of her desk. A raindrop ran down my forehead, along the bridge of my nose and landed on Peg's neatly stacked 'outgoing' mail.

The room was a blur. I put my glasses into my breast pocket and dropped the lens in with a plink after them.

J. stayed on the phone and her glance, when it came up, passed over me as it might an uninteresting newspaper headline. She laughed into the phone; a strained and high-pitched laugh.

'She's talking to Paris,' I was informed. Peg said it with a smug professional tone that made me want to bat her off her stool.

'Don't forget,' J. said into the receiver. 'We don't make the films here. We just show them.' She lit a cigarette. Two lights, one green and one blue, blinked on the phone. I found that very unsettling. As if two people had slipped invisibly into the room and queued up in front of me.

She stretched her body like a cat. 'We'll pay the plane fare, hotel, meals and a per diem for *ten* days. Not the bar bill. That's yours.'

The conversation seemed to trail off but then, at the point of logical extinction, it hummed back to life. By now, it looked as if I was going to hang around. Peg Leg sensed the privacy of their moment was threatened. She couldn't relax, kept throwing quick looks my way, the last one prolonged and small eyed, accompanied by a sigh as soft as a butterfly.

I was definitely spoiling things. Finally she dropped all pretense of civility and stared hotly. The audience was over, didn't I understand that? Like a cow stuck in the middle of the road I was only holding up traffic.

And J., between her soothing cajoleries, knew I was there. She cupped her hand over the telephone and whispered, 'Put him down for five days; Unifrance can pay the rest. Let them sort it out among themselves.'

I opened my mouth but she resumed the conversation. Peg's beady peepers climbed up the side of my cheek like two damp slugs. I felt suddenly very tired and I wanted to say, 'Peggy, if you say one word to me, I'm going to rip up your typing and break the stamp machine.'

But I didn't. I didn't say anything.

She was on the verge of saying something; you could almost see her tongue flick out to test the air. But finding it hostile she returned to her typing.

'Tell J.,' I whispered, 'I'll pick up Fran after school. Tomorrow. As planned.'

Sucking up. Being a good guy. What a decent chap. A terrible fight but still assumes his responsibilities as a father. I think I was hoping for her approval, that maybe she'd say something nice about me after I left. But no such luck. Her head bobbed up and down with mechanical cheerfulness. She didn't answer and that annoyed me.

'Did you hear me?' I asked.

'Yes,' she said with fatigue.

'Then why don't you answer me? You don't need to be rude.'

Her round, nickel face popped up looking bewildered. J. clicked down the phone, rose without a word.

'I'll get Franny tomorrow,' I said. She didn't reply and in a moment I was alone in the office, staring out the window at the rain. I was waiting for her to come back, like the old days.

I dallied a bit longer. She might come in and with a laugh.... But, as some sage pointed out, there comes a time when she doesn't come after you anymore. It's hard to believe that she'll let you leave, or let the moment stay like this, unresolved, jagged.

There was nothing to do but go out and get drunk. I left the office and looked up and down the hall; she was somewhere, waiting for me to leave. I took the red elevator downstairs and she wasn't in the lobby. I went back outside, feeling sorry for myself, really tragic, full of self disgust. And oddly heartbroken, like a fresh wound.

'You shouldn't have let me leave.' An old refrain, something she hurled at me years ago when she stormed out of my university residence because I told her the bed was too small for two....

I went into the Circus, choked down a couple of depth charges. But it wasn't the right night for a voyage so I said fuck it and went home.

Chapter Three

I lived in an ugly house on an ugly street. There were no trees and no children. The houses were squat, two storeyed, with phoney yellow-brick shingles. It was as if some demented contractor had sawed off all the third floors up and down the length of our humourless street.

A bonehead named Norton owned it. He was a journalist, an old friend of J.'s, natch. He wrote dreary, constipated drama reviews. But he worked all the time. He took a kind of crazed pride in never relaxing. I'd lie in bed and I'd hear him typing, sometimes all night. It was like an audible conscience.

It was a gloomy, gloomy apartment. Its only window, situated above the bed, looked across a sunless walkway. The bedroom was always dark, a good place to have a hangover. You could loll about in the darkness without having to confront the obscenity of diamond-clear sunlight and the knowledge that you'd blown another day.

Even the birds stayed away from my window sill.

I painted the walls battleship grey. I thought it might

look modern. 'It lacks a woman's touch,' pronounced a doe-eyed undergraduate as she slipped out one morning. She was right of course. Except it wasn't her touch it lacked. The point was it didn't matter. Whenever I needed a cocoon, I had it.

There was one thing about the place I really hated: the bathroom was in the basement, down a set of scaffold-like stairs carpeted the colour of baby poop. They were a nightmare at three in the morning, so I used to piss in the kitchen sink and as time went on and I began to despise Norton more and more I fantasized about the piss rusting the pipes, that years after my departure the entire plumbing system would collapse.

Shortly after I arrived home that night, there was a solid, unapologetic knocking on my door. It was Norton. He handed me my mail, a gesture which made me immediately suspicious.

'What's up?' I asked in a peculiar voice.

'A couple of things actually. We have to raise the rent.' He paused, then added ominously, 'approval came through today. You see we really have to generate more income.'

'How much?'

'A hundred dollars a month, I'm afraid. I wasn't expecting them to grant it really.'

'But they did?'

'They did indeed.' He shrugged with feigned resignation.

'I can't afford a hundred dollars more, Norton,' I said, with a simplicity that surprised even me.

'How much can you afford then? Not that it makes any difference.' With anyone else I might have laughed, but Norton wasn't kidding. It really *didn't* make any difference.

He went on. 'Look, I'm satisfied with you as a tenant. Our children get along and that's certainly a consideration. But we must have more income.'

I was starting to slide into panic. 'I like living here, Norton. The neighbours know my name. I don't want to move.'

'I understand that.'

'Maybe there's something I could do. Odd jobs. Babysitting.' I could hardly picture myself in overalls with a hammer in my belt. And neither could Norton.

'It's the income,' he said sadly. 'The darn old income.'

'I don't know what I'm going to do.'

'Find another hundred dollars I guess.'

'I'll have to think about it.'

He looked cunningly at me. Whatever he'd planned, it was going perfectly.

'Would you mind if I showed someone your apartment, just in case you decide to leave? They could come over tonight.'

'I'm not going to leave, Norton. I'm just going to think about it.' He looked deliberately and theatrically perplexed, and my eyes watered with humiliation. I knew I was contradicting myself but I just wanted him to shut the door and go back upstairs.

'Are you feeling all right?' he asked. For a second I thought he might feel my brow for a fever. 'You look a little tense.'

'That's true, Norton. I'm wrapped pretty tight today.'

'I'll be upstairs,' he said and shut the door.

I started to tidy up my apartment. I worked myself into a rage. There's nothing quite like housework to get your mind racing, trot out those old feuds, reargue old quarrels, make those points you wished you'd made back then. After an hour I felt like stuffing my mattress out the window. I must have been waiting for J. to call. But she didn't. And the more I waited, the more incensed I got. Not just at her, but at her ass-licking secretary, at Norton, at myself for sucking around J. so much, at my dentist who had overbilled me, at my lawyer – I forgot why – and a girl named Raissa who had told somebody who had told somebody who had told me that I was afraid of success and that's why I left my wife.

I had a lot of scores to settle that night, or so it felt, and sweeping the dust kittens from under the refrigerator wasn't giving me the satisfaction I needed.

The phone rang once when I was scrubbing the toilet bowl. But it stopped before I got there.

I fell asleep while it was still light and woke up suddenly and violently shortly after one-thirty. There's nothing like waking up like that. It's the loneliest, most ghostly of feelings. It makes you feel that you did something terrible back there and you've been paying for it ever since. Your loneliness is so strong it's almost palpable; it pushes you into your clothes, along the street; it makes you break into a run, to run back to someone you loved at nineteen, flip through an old address book, an old phone directory, call a friend who knew her, to arrive breathless at her door. You try and slip in the back door, pretend you're nostalgic, pretend you're in the neighbourhood, pretend anything except that you feel a hundred years old and you're dying to go to bed with an old lover because she used to make you feel like magic.

I sat up and looked at the phone. To see if it was working I dialed the operator. I wanted a cigarette – it was the second time that day. I was waiting for the phone to ring and it hadn't. I thought I'd go back to sleep and get up early and get to the office before eight-thirty, before everybody arrived and the phones started ringing and then J. and I could talk about this thing, this 'we should have got someone else' business.

Lying on my bed, staring at a long crack which ran the length of the ceiling, I rehearsed what I'd say, how she'd answer. But she didn't call. Around three o'clock I was still awake and starting to fume. I thought she must really not give a fuck at all. She knew me well enough to know that an argument like that would tear a piece off me a foot long. Regardless of who 'won.' The older I get, the more raw flesh those moments scrape off. You get obsessed with things that used to fly right by you. It's harder to get to sleep when you've left it jagged with someone. I don't know how I've gotten so much weaker, so ready to acquiesce, so distrustful of myself. I don't know how it happened but at some point I started believing the shitty things I heard about myself. I don't know, but I used to jump hurdles to give myself the benefit of the doubt.

Anyway, tomorrow. Tomorrow in the morning we'll talk about the fuse and then about the fuse box. And then we'll get onto the book. Everyone says it's a beauty. And I know it reads well. There'll be mistakes but there are mistakes every year. The editor before me referred to Michelangelo Antonioni as the 'greatest living amateur in Italian film.' He meant 'auteur.' Now that was a typo and they didn't 'get someone else' after that.

And speaking of typos, how about mistaking Fassbinder's *The Marriage of Maria Braun* for *The Marriage of* Eva *Braun*.

And they still didn't 'get someone else.'

If only I could get a good night's sleep. If only I could stop running and rerunning that tape through my head.... 'Get someone else, the book's a mess ... why don't you just go?'

And the final image of myself, bovine, floppy eared, a cowbell around my neck, staring stupidly into space as the car horns blared from both sides of the dusty road.

Near five in the morning I noticed a piece of paper lying on the carpet across the room, just in front of the door. I was surprised not to have noticed it before. It was a simple message and I laughed before finishing it. It said: '*It is my intention to apply for a Spirits Licence at the next convening in Savanna-la-Mar.*'

It was from Dexter. There was no signature but I knew he'd been working on the coal tugs all summer, that his time was up; he'd jumped ship in Toronto with pockets bursting with five months pay, and – most important – he'd headed back to Jamaica.

And he wanted company.

I went back to bed and nearly fell asleep but then, just like that, I started thinking about John Lennon. I lay in bed thinking about him and then I heard that ghostly piano from 'Imagine' and then it was six and then six-thirty and I knocked over the alarm clock when I reached for it; it lay on its back, its wan, idiot face looking up at me like it'd been KO'd.

And fuck me I'll be tired in the morning, more tired and weaker than I was today.

It started again. I couldn't stop the hysterical, forward march of my imagination, my thoughts cluttered with glittering junk, ditties, snatches of conversation.

The rain in Spain falls mainly on the plain, the rain in Spain, in Spain. And you lie there and you realize that your fists are clenched and that trying to fall asleep is like trying to run through waist-high water.

'Did you know that earthworms are translaterally symmetrical?' I waited all my life to answer that question. I'm the first to raise my arm.

'No, sir.' I pause, waiting for the attention of the class.

'No, sir, worms are bilaterally symmetrical.'

What a bright lad.

'Yes sir.'

'The rain in Spain falls mainly on the plain.'

'If you're sick, go to the hospital.'

'And if I'm not?'

'Then you must get up and go to school.'

'But I don't feel well.'

'Hey, hey Johnny. Can you come out to play? Hey Johnny, can you come out to play?'

And just when I gave up on the idea of sleeping, when I turned on the bedside lamp and lay there, still staring at the crack, thinking I'll get up and have a shower and two cups of coffee, take a couple of codeine pills, I'll just lie here a few more seconds, under the blankets and then I got warmer and warmer and my thoughts stopped racing and I didn't think about Lennon anymore or J. or the phone ringing ... and the crack in the ceiling looked like a long and graceful S ... and I could hear my daughter explain to me that it wasn't an S, that it was an 'l,' a small 'l.' In her keen and excited voice she explained and reex-plained how the letters were different and then I stopped thinking and the thoughts came by them-selves, acted themselves out, coming no longer from my will but from somewhere else, and I watched them passively. And then I knew I was asleep or sinking into sleep where nothing, no thought or image or memory could stop me. I was sinking soundlessly, without a sense of motion, deeper and deeper until I settled, warm and insulated, until I came to a graceful halt at the very bottom of my dream.

I dreamt about Franny and the two of us standing on the cliffs in Jamaica. Dexter was across the patio. The sun is an inch over the smoking water and Franny's face drips with gold light. She basks in the light and I stand beside her, a scarecrow, black rags flapping disconsolately in the evening breeze. The lights flicker in the boat houses up and down the shore line.

And then her voice, breathless with excitement, a voice as fresh as strawberries. 'Look everybody, look. Daddy caught a fish!'

Chapter Four

A crisp knocking woke me up. It was eight-thirty in the morning. I was sick with fatigue, my jaw ached as if I'd drunk a bottle of mescal and fallen down the stairs. To make matters worse I'd forgotten to open the windows. The pilot light on the stove had gone out. There was the faint aroma of gas and I had a crashing headache. Handsome Norton was there like a glass of freshly squeezed orange juice. Doubtless he'd been up since six, fixing a screen or tearing up tile in the basement.

'I'm sorry to tell you this,' he began with his favourite shrug, 'but the rent raise is retroactive. I was going to tell you last night but I didn't have the heart. You seemed so distraught.'

I waited speechless.

'In a word it means that you owe three hundred dollars as well as this month's rent.'

From there things escalated very quickly.

'You should have your wife deal with your tenants,' I said.

'We were wondering,' he continued patiently, 'when we could count on your cheque?'

'Did you hear me? I said you should have your wife deal with your tenants.'

Then he did a bizarre thing. He put his hand on my shoulder, paternally, squeezed, and for a second I thought he was trying to scare me. That's all it took. I discovered long ago that I'd rather have someone punch me in the face or even beat the hell out of me than scare me like that. I felt a shot of adrenalin through my veins. I hadn't meant for it to go this far. But it had and I took careful aim. I knew I had only one clean shot and if it didn't work, he'd be all over me. I aimed at his right eye, right below his glasses. I wanted to give him a shiner. I wanted him to have to explain to everyone why his eye was black, explain and explain for three weeks and every time he'd think of me.

I let go a good one, one of those beauties where you've got nothing to lose, the range is just right and there's that proper snap in your arm just before you make contact. Norton flew back out of the doorway up against the wall. But he didn't go down. Not even close. He came back off the wall. I had about three seconds to do something spectacular, something to stop him in his tracks. I didn't have a gun or I would have shot him. I smashed my fist through the glass door; it shattered. I pulled out a six-inch shard of glass, jabbed it into my forearm and yanked it. That stopped him. We stared at each other in silence. He was frozen, his eyes glued to my arm. He couldn't take his eyes off it. I was breathing heavily through my teeth and blood dripped onto the carpet.

The next moments, like the rest of the day, have little continuity. They seem now like slashes of colour, tableaux that are seared into my imagination. Indeed it was as if my life had roared into a furious and obsessive overdrive. Three hours later, I had twelve hundred dollars in my pocket. Franny and I were on a jet to Jamaica.

But of those hours before, I recall only images: a splash of bloody fingerprints on the telephone, a handful of bloodied keys. I remember wiping my arm the length of the white kitchen wall; it left a brilliant red streak. Terrifying anger. The taxi to the hospital, a nauseating crawl through early-morning traffic. The young Oriental doctor: I sat, catatonic, staring straight ahead at the gleaming bottles and chrome while he sewed me up like a stuffed doll.

The race to the pawn shops; cluttered, junked-up windows, guitars, stereo sets, silver mugs, initialled snifters, television sets. 'WE BUY PAWN TICKETS, GOLD BOUGHT AND SOLD.'

My arm throbbing, a small circle of blood spreading through the bandage, the size of a dime, then a nickel, then a quarter. I had a ring to sell. A two-carat diamond ring, a diamond as big as the Ritz my mother used to say. It was the last remnant of my estate and my family. It was worth six. I wanted two.

'Borrowing or selling?' the man said across the stall.

'Selling.'

'Can't give you more than a thousand.'

'Done.'

I went to the corner. The adrenalin was really pumping now as the idea formed itself. I telephoned my nephew. I needed more money. I hadn't seen him for three months, not since we cleaned out the music department of my old high school. A good haul it was; it took us three trips and made the newspapers. He was sitting on it for me.

'Martin,' I said, 'we've got to dump that stuff. I'm in a bit of trouble.'

'Today?'

'Absolutely.'

'Don't you think it's a bit soon?'

'Look, they ... I was just there. I sold the ring. They don't bother with the serial numbers if you're selling. Give them somebody else's name.'

'I'm still on probation.'

I'd forgotten. Six months before, he got drunk and had tried to boost a horse dink of Kohlbassa from his neighbourhood delicatessen. He got caught.

'I'm in a real bind here,' I said.

'It's going to look a little odd, isn't it,' he asked me, 'if I pull in there with three saxophones, a half-dozen stratocasters and a mixing board?'

He laughed and I knew we'd be all right.

'Sell as much as you can. I really need the money.'

He hung up. An hour later we had a drink at the Circus and he gave me another four hundred.

'What's wrong with your arm?' he asked.

I started to tell him the story but he cut me off.

'Don't tell me the rest,' he cautioned. 'Then I won't be lying when I say I don't know where you've gone.'

The next sharp memory is of Franny, her blue eyes looking at me in the airplane. She had a blue-black crescent below her right eye.

'How'd you get the shiner?'

'I ran into a dog at school.'

She knew I wasn't being straight with her; and she'd known it from the moment I picked her up at school. She was suspicious but polite about it. But this business with the airplane was a bit much even for a five year old.

I ordered a double Scotch and used it to wash down a couple of percodans.

Sitting right ahead of us was a big-headed, American Legion type with a nasty, flat-top haircut, a red face and a veiny nose. I hated him immediately and it was reciprocal.

While Fran was in the bathroom he raised his huge, tulip head over the seat.

'How'd your little girl get that shiner?'

'At school.'

'Yeah?'

'A dog stuck his nose in her face.'

He gave me one hard look and squeezed back down in the seat. The full thrust didn't hit me for a moment. Then a stewardess came by with a can of cold ginger ale, bent over Fran and let out a little gasp of surprise.

'Oh dear. What happened to your eye?'

It occurred to me later that there had been nothing accusatorial in her tone, no assumption of guilt but it hit a raw nerve.

'A dog did it.'

My American Legion friend stared between the seats, then leant over to his wife. I caught a glimpse of myself in the window. I was white and sweating. And I looked crazy. I was hot, but because of the bandage, I didn't want to take my jacket off. The blood stain had stopped growing. It sat in the centre of my forearm the size of a poppy. But it was dark now and I knew I'd stopped bleeding. I gagged on the last of the scotch and ordered a vodka tonic. 'With a lemon,' I added.

Fran liked that. She wanted to play with the lemon.

'We can't play with a lemon in the plane. It'll make a mess.'

She looked at me in a thoughtful, adult way. 'Why

didn't you tell J. we were going on an airplane?'

'I wanted to surprise her.'

'What kind of toy would you like?' she asked.

'We don't have any toys here.'

'Pretend.'

'No,' I said. Something was starting to sink. The adrenalin was wearing off. By now J. would have called my apartment; she'd assume I'd taken our daughter to the park before dinner.

'What kind of toy would you like?' she repeated.

'None.'

'Why not?'

'Because, Fran, I'm not a kid. I'm too big to play,' I snapped.

'Do you have a mom?'

'Yes, I have a mom.'

'Then you *are* a kid. What kind of a toy do you want?'

'A spider,' I said. 'Let's have a spider.'

I moved out of J.'s apartment in Chinatown when Fran was a year and a half old. After that – and for as long as she was single – I used to drop around to the apartment in the late afternoons and the three of us would have dinner and then we bathed Fran and then I left. One evening I was sitting in a chair beside the bathtub and Franny was splashing and nattering and singing little tuneless bars. I don't remember where J. was but at one point I realized that I was late, that I had to go. And I wanted to stay with Fran, I really did, but I also really wanted to go.

'Franny,' I said gently, 'I have to go.' And she stretched out a little cream-coloured arm and pulled the plug and I felt such tenderness for her, such extraordinary love. I leaned over and kissed her, kissed her on the top of her blond head.

She was absorbed with the water whirling down the drain and she didn't seem to take any notice. But then, without looking at me, she asked, 'Why are you kissing me?'

And the question, the evenness with which she asked it, rocked me.

'Because I love you.'

'No, you're kissing me because you're leaving.'

It came like an electric shock. I'd been caught in a false moment and without so much as directing her eyes at me she'd unmasked me. I had kissed her because I did feel guilty; the hand was hers, unmistakably, and I knew that from then on she'd always be just ahead of me, that I'd inevitably end up running behind her, carrying last month's assumptions like last year's snow suit.

I ordered another vodka.

'Will J. meet us at the airport?'

'No, I told you. It's a surprise.'

'I don't want a surprise.' She was slipping into teary

confusion and fatigue. 'I want J. to meet us at the airport.'

'But I'm here. I'll be with you.'

'But I want J.'

'Stop that. You're making me ... why do you do this? It's the same at school. You always make me feel like a disappointment because I'm not J. It's not fair.'

She fell silent and glubbed quietly.

'Fran,' I whispered angrily, 'it's not my fault that I'm not your mother.'

'Whose fault is it then?'

'These questions are driving me crazy. I don't know what to do.'

My arm was starting to throb and I got up and went into the bathroom with my shoulder bag to change the dressing. Inside, when I clicked the bolt, the light flashed a sickly hospital bright and a green face looked back at me. My arm had started to bleed again; I sat down on the toilet seat and I started to think about Fran and her tub again. Those moments, they happen and they sink right through you like depth charges. And then someday, sometimes years ahead, suddenly they're there again, when you're not looking for them – in a restaurant or the back of a taxi or passing a store window at Christmas, suddenly they're there, right in front of you, as vivid, as palpable as when they first happened. And then they go off.

I took two more codeine pills. It was the last of them; they were burning out the bottom of my stomach and my head was starting to ring. I put a new dressing on, washed my face and tried to think about Jamaica, the sun on my back. If only I could get there, could get to Harris's hotel up in the cliffs, if only I could lie down in that white room, just lie down and sleep ... in the morning we'd go for a swim and when my head cleared a bit and my arm didn't hurt so much, then I'd think what to do.

When I came out of the bathroom, the Legionnaire was bent over Fran, whispering to her. She wasn't looking at him; her head was down and she fiddled with a brass button on her belt. It made me instantly furious but – and this seemed truly alarming – it felt like I'd run out of gas.

'That's quite a shiner,' the bull neck said, eyeing my shoulder bag and then me. Christ, I thought, he thinks I'm a drug addict, that I've just whacked up a barrel of smack in the can and now I'll beat up my kid again.

'I don't want to dwell on it,' I said.

'Still, lucky she didn't lose an eye. Did he bite her or what?'

The vodka arrived; Franny sipped a cold ginger ale through a straw and listened.

'Why don't you ask her?'

'I did. She says she doesn't know.'

He'd had a couple of drinks since the flight took off – rye, judging from the smell, and there was a querulous tone to his voice. Somewhere a small heating unit had ignited in that enormous head, the beginnings of an ugly mood. And his wife, who said nothing, had the look, the thin-lipped look of someone who has learned the hard way to keep her peace.

He left. Fran looked over. 'Were you crying because your arm hurts?'

'I wasn't crying.'

We were silent for a while.

'Where does your mommy live?'

'My mom died, Fran. She lived a long, long time and then she got old and died.'

'Will you go to heaven?'

'Probably not,' I said, 'but let's have lunch anyway.'

Chapter Five

Montego Bay: green island in a blue, blue sea. The plane clears the ocean, slows to a halt in front of a glittering white one-level terminal. The heat runs up the stairs, bursts into the cabin when they open the doors. These people can't wait. This is a holiday; the wheels don't hit the shimmering tarmac before they're out of their seats like excited children, splitting the seams of the plane.

A long, smooth corridor, down which Fran and I swoosh as if on roller skates; it spills into a central, circus-sized arena; it bustles with gold bags and tennis rackets, the whole thing swimming in heat and smooth cement and madras shirts, Hawaiian shirts, flour sack shirts, Mexican cotton shirts, T-bone hats from Dallas, Ivy League hats, straw hats from Oaxaca, T-shirts from New York, Puerto Rico ... and all those white limbs and white bodies, racks of grey winter skin lined up like cattle at the polished wooden customs booths.

'What is the purpose of your journey, sir?'

'I say, boy, what the fuck do you think the purpose

is? I'm here to have a hell of a time and you're keepin'
me from it.'

'Well Franny,' I say, steadying myself on a porter's
cart, 'this is it. Welcome to paradise.'

She's stunned by the heat, the colour, the activity.

'I told you, Fran; the trees are so green here you can
hear them sing.'

In front of me, a guy in his early thirties with a day's
growth and a weak chin is complaining. He's standing
in his stall – it could be an abattoir – and he says they
bent the frame on his bicycle. The customs official
doesn't see the damage. The guy is getting madder and
madder. He wants action; he wants somebody's ass
kicked; he wants the nigger that fucked his bike
brought out here right now and castrated.

The official, dusting a fly from his immaculate blue
epaulette, directs him to a booth in the back of the
arena. It's marked baggage and there's no one in it.

'You can register your complaint there.'

'But there's no one in it.'

'There will be soon.'

'But I'll have to lose my place in line.'

Mr. Customs shakes his head. He looks at his
watch. He's lost interest in the conversation and shifts
his hat.

'What can we do?'

The guy pushes his way through customs, holding
his cycle aloft like the body of Caesar.

'By the way,' the gringo whines over his shoulder, 'where can I cash travellers' cheques?' The customs man smiles and a group of black guys leap out of nowhere with offers of black-market money, two dollars to one, one dollar to fifty cents, a cab ride, a limousine ride, a hearse ride, fifty bucks Jamaican into the centre of town, fifty U.S. to Negril. He's like a carcass and they're over him like buzzards.

Like a bad hallucination, the American Legionnaire clomps up, bags and wife in tow. I'm not the only one to have had too many drinks on the plane. He winks at me, remembers who I am, and scowls. He's thinking about the black eye; he'd just love to take me aside and thrash the daylights out of me, blast out his ugly rage for a just cause.

'Hey little girl,' he begins but Franny is smarter than he is; she can smell trouble, that something's off here. She doesn't say anything. She looks at him and says nothing and doubt crosses his big face; suddenly he's not sure and he reaches out his hand to pat her on the head, as if she were a dog, and she darts back, ducking under his hand.

The Legionnaire's caught with his hand out and no one there. The kid doesn't want him touching her and that's clear. He looks around to see who's noticed. His wife did and my heart goes out to her because, later, she'll have to pay for that one too.

'This is paradise, Fran,' I say and run my hand

across her blond hair. She looks up at me with eyes the colour of the sea and for a moment it seems it's going to turn out all right. Just us. Even my arm has stopped throbbing.

A tray of drinks is stuck under my nose. Dark rum punch. I take one for me and one for Fran. I'm grappling for our birth certificates. Franny wants to present hers. I throw back the rum punch; it's warm, gooey, but I take another off the tray and toss it back. I'm delaying the white rum now, the overproof, the fire water, the bottle that explodes when it hits the floor. Not yet. Wait a bit more. Just to get settled, calm down, get a handle on things, make a plan, make a phone call. I finish the second rum punch; it sends a wave of nausea through me. The Legionnaire is behind me, his angry red eyes squeezing out of his face. It's true though; I am behaving exactly as a frantic, guilt-stricken father might. Franny takes a taste from the rum punch, hands me the plastic cup, wrinkling up her face. 'You can have it,' she says.

The heat, the strain, the liquor are taking effect. Time moves forward in flashes like a stop-action photograph. People and things are caught in different postures, frozen. I've got to stop drinking and clear my head but I know I won't. Can Fran and I simply fly to Jamaica and live happily ever after? The reality of the situation is catching up but I've got a full head of steam. I'm a mile from my barn but I can smell the oats already. Get to the hotel, get into the white, wind-swept room, watch the ceiling spin and then slowly, like toffee on a hot day, everything will slow down, settle into the cracks and seal fast. In the meantime kiddies, I'll watch the bags. You chase after the lady with the tray of drinks. Fetch your pop one of them rum punches, okay?

Franny sets off among the people and the colours and the salty air and steps tentatively across the putty-like green cement. She looks back to see if I'm watching and it occurs to me that her limbs aren't white like those of the adults around her; they're a different colour, white without the rot. I say to myself, stay off the overproof. Stay with the dark rum; it'll get you drunk but it won't make you crazy. I've got to buy her some shorts and I've got to see she stays out of the sun and I've got to avoid the overproof.

'Pssssst.' Through the white portals in the reception area a black head peeks in. Like a caricature, he rolls his eyes, grins and says 'Ganja?'

I shake my head.

He says, 'American money? You want some change today? American dollars?'

'Red Stripe, cold pop, soursap juice?'

'How about a Cadillac?'

'Yeah man.'

Franny crawls behind my legs; she can't resist look-ing. The black head looks down forbiddingly, then smiles.

'Yeah man.' The head disappears.

Fran steps out. 'Will J. meet us here?'

My attention snaps back to her.

'No, but she'll be here.'

It's got to get better. How long before she stops ask-ing?

It's obvious now what I'm going to do. I'm on a treadmill and I know in advance where it's taking me. Just let it go, like a long smooth escalator, a hundred yards long, running dead flat beside the hot pavement. Stay awake, stand still, go to sleep, jump up and down. No matter.

Eyes the colour of blueberries; they look up again. Of all this afternoon's reshuffled moments, this tableau I'll remember forever. And me, white-faced, ashen with fatigue, white with the loss of blood, white with anger, white with frustration. Frustration because you never loved anyone as much as you ima-gined you could, that somewhere, still, you're waiting for it to happen and time is moving on. You're not the new kid on the block anymore. There's no reason to believe that the next one will be different from the last one. You can't keep practising forever. Maybe it goes like this; maybe it was J. And if that's the case then it wasn't a question of missing the train. They tore down the station before I even packed. A failure at loving and therefore, logically, a failure at everything else. And after that, what else is there to talk about? What else is there to be good at? Goodbye Jamaica, the air is stagnant, unbreathable. It blows through the jet turbines, over the tarmac; it blows, festers over the people and shirts and hats and bags; it blows over the island like an open sore and back out to sea ... everyone in this airport is white, ashen, defeated, and so am I.

And here I am in paradise with a stolen child. It's turning weepy, teary, old, hacked-up verses from Apollinaire: '... Te serre le gosier, comme si tu ne devais jamais plus être aimé....'

As if you'll never be loved again.

When J. and I crammed for that Chaucer exam, that soft spring morning, the two of us, all night, decks of Rothman's and sweet tea, we never, even as a joke, imagined our lives might end up here, in this small, pinched retaliatory attic.

'Psssssst.' The voice comes again. 'American money?'

The child says: 'We don't have any money.' The spell is broken and we inch forward to the customs booth.

'How is your eye?' I ask and she touches a pink forefinger to the bluish bump and pushes ever so gently.

'Good.'

What will we do tomorrow? Tomorrow afternoon? We'll go to the sea and walk on the beach ... and time will go by and this nightmare, will it pass too? How, exactly, is everything going to be all right?

'No more street for you,' the Jamaicans say when they see you with a child. It means the fun's over, the running's through and evenings now you stay at home with the little one. Is that what I planned? And what about her mother? Where exactly do I start? Do I say: 'Listen I'm sorry about this but Franny and I have gone to Jamaica and I'm not sure when we'll be back. And by the way, I'm so drunk the walls are dripping blood.'

No, that wouldn't do.

'Come and get her. Come and take her home.'

How did it ever get so fucked?

Fran is looking up again. 'Who are you talking to?' she asks.

And now we're in the customs booth.

'Destination?' the man asks.

'To see my mommy,' Fran answers.

'She's staying in a hotel in Negril.'

'Anything to declare?' he asks, looking down at her.

She stares at him blankly, undaunted, waiting for an explanation.

And then they both laugh, as if at the same joke. I can't guess what it is.

Outside into the full, hot sun, the van drivers, cab drivers, money changers, ganja dealers, honey oil dealers, beer vendors, all milling, crowding. They tug your sleeve; they whisper in your ear; but they're familiar and they make me feel safe, at home. Nobody pushes, nobody offers you his sister or a blow job or a donkey fuck on the outskirts of town. They want to make a little bread. One of them in a pair of red wool pants – like the Mexicans, they think only fags wear shorts – makes a bee line for me. He's threading his way through the crowd. Tall, black and angular he slides around Franny, addresses me nose to nose. He's got something for me; he knows I'm the man.

'What is it?'

'A ride, sir. A ride to Negril.'

The others take up the cry but there's a lot of us white folks. The chinless one with the bike is arguing; he brays ineffectually. A Jamaican cabbie is pretending to get pissed off but he enjoys the spectacle, this white guy turning purple with rage, his veins standing out like chords on his neck.

'Fifty dollars,' Red Pants shouts at me. 'You and your daughter, two persons....' He holds up two fingers in case I'm not following.... 'Fifty dollars, sah!'

'When do we leave?'

He gestures towards a brand-new grey Volkswagen van. It's a beauty. It's also empty.

'We go right now.'

That means half an hour. I crook my finger at him. He comes closer. He's getting agitated; it's taking too long to sew this up; he should be on to the next sale by now. He can't help himself; his eyes work the crowd. Everything he says sounds like a speech. It's totally insincere but he's too busy to even pretend. His eyes leave mine, dart around the crowd. He's lining up the next one as he puts this one to bed.

'I've been here before,' I say softly.

He pretends to be impressed; he still can't keep his eyes on me.

'Yeah man, I know. I can tell from the experience in your voice.'

He's bullshitting me but I like it.

'I paid ten dollars.'

He pauses, makes a decision, then bears down.

'Twenty-five for two.'

He has just caught sight of the angry cyclist. For a second he's torn. Should he concentrate on me, a hard sell, or should he let this one go and concentrate on a real target?

'Fifteen,' I say, 'and we'll wait.'

'Twenty U.S.,' he adds, 'but don't tell anyone.'

'For both?'

'Yeah man.'

He's itchy; he wants to go. It's a deal and he pushes off after the cyclist who's just broken off negotiations and is standing alone, fuming, under the hot sun, the sea behind him. There's no trace of colour on his face except the white peak of anger still smouldering on his cheeks.

I throw the suitcase into the van and Franny and I climb in near the back. I want to hear the bartering so I lower the side window and lean my ear unobtrusively in their direction. It's as I suspected; the bicycle man is making a big score. He's talking Red Pants down from fifty U.S. to forty.

Franny is frozen with interest. To my right the van door slides open and a fat man with a New York Yankees baseball hat slides in leisurely. He's got a Red Stripe in his hand; it's ice cold. There's frost on the outside and it makes my mouth water. The fat man has a round face, friendly and open. He's from the Deep South and he looks around the van in a relaxed manner, pulls out the neck of his T-shirt to let out some of the steam, puts his arm up on the seat and says, simply, 'yep.' There it is; that easy, leisurely accent, that sittin' by the bayou, watchin' the Mississippi roll on by.

'I been here four times,' he says, taking a pull on his beer. 'I know what I like and I come here to get it.' Red Pants is assisting the cyclist to strap his vehicle on the roof of the van. 'Those straps can't possibly hold,' he says impatiently. 'Can't you see that? One bump and it'll be gone. That's a six hundred dollar machine. I rode across the Pyrenees on that.'

'Yeah man.' Red Pants doesn't have the forty dollars in his hand yet so he'll put up with this a while longer. Besides, you can tell he's a veteran of the Pyrenees himself.

The Southerner stretches a cool-palmed hand across the aisle and I shake it. 'Otto,' he says. He looks back out the window towards the Blue Mountains. One huge, verdant wave, speckled with white, glittering houses.

'Pretty goddamn close to paradise,' he says. 'Y'all been here before?'

'Yep.'

'I been here four times.'

Fran stares at him with unabashed fascination. She's never heard that accent before.

'You're gonna be one brown little girl when you leave here.'

Red Pants has clambered onto the roof with a clutch of rope.

Otto pokes his head out the window. 'Any chance of hearin' some music?'

There's no please, no forced politeness. It's a request of remarkable gentility.

More sighs of impatience from the cyclist. His girlfriend is standing nervously in the shade under a bright red awning. Red Pants takes off his belt and uses it to fasten the bicycle, then clambers down. The cyclist crawls in front of us with a disgusted look: 'A belt! I don't fuckin' believe these guys.'

Otto smiles. He's not taking anyone's side. This is a man who knows how to enjoy himself; no point in gettin' ruffled over a belt or a bicycle or five bucks or whether the music comes on now or later. It's all the same.

Franny catches sight of something and jumps excitedly out of her seat. She slips across the aisle and onto Otto's seat. It's a hat vendor, wearing three straw hats with gaudy ribbons and Jamaica sewn across the brim.

In her excitement she leans against Otto. Neither seems to notice.

'You tried the overproof?' Otto asks me.

'I want a hat,' the child chirps. The vendor has taken off the top hat and waves it enticingly back and forth. He has yellow eyes.

'There are better hats than that, honey,' Otto says. 'Last year I bought a bottle of overproof for my friends back home. Known them all my life, grew up together, went to college together. We sat down, the four of us, and I swear to God it's the only time I remember when a bottle lasted more than one sitting.' Pause. 'Wicked, but the only way to fly.'

He doesn't wait for my answer but adjusts the rim on his hat, slowly, thoughtfully, savouring the memory, the après-goût of his story. It doesn't matter what I say. The story is the point. And now, momentarily, he's peacefully at sea on it, somewhere calm on a summer's night. The van door opens again; a couple with a small baby climb in, smiling, nervous about the child, the heat, the two-hour bumpy ride to Negril. They're followed by a long black-haired Israeli girl in her early twenties. She's stunning. She carries an enormous, gleaming silver tape deck. She's an old traveller, this one. I met her two years ago. We both pretend not to recognize each other. She's still running the same scam with the tape deck. She buys it in Canada, sells it for Jamaican money, then claims it was stolen and pockets the insurance money. It's how she finances the trip. I try to remember her name. Is it Jesse? I can't remember. She's got terrific tits. I remember that much and I check to see if they're still there. Indeed they are and neither Otto nor I can take our eyes off them.

It never stops, I think, and I'm sort of hoping that tape deck, big and shiny like it is, with all those knobs and lights, I'm hoping it'll attract Franny's attention, that maybe she'll push up the aisle for a peek – pave the way for a graceful reintroduction.

I feel like a deep-sea fisherman, trolling the gulf with my child at the end of the line.

But no luck. Franny wants her hat. She insists. I refuse; the Israeli turns enough in her seat to knock the wind out of me and smiles a smile full of large, white teeth.

'So you really *do* have a daughter,' she says.

The van starts. We're off. We pull onto a dazzling crushed quartz road; the sea's behind us now as we tuck in at the bottom of the hills, turn right, winding slowly up through towns called Sandy Bay, Hopewell, Green Bay, Lucea – laundry lines sparkle with pinks and oranges and whites. The hillside is dotted with yellow government houses; you can feel the heat hovering above the aluminum siding. Cemetery stones mark the way and the sunlight shimmers pale silver off the road. Like old silverware.

I remember taking this trip at night once, coal black, star lit, the villas glowing from the hillside like corrupt rubies.

We rattle over a wooden panelled bridge; the road becomes tar black, oozes between shoulder-high canefields, cuts through red rock. A rusted bulldozer cooks in the sun next to a pink, faded one-level house, an abandoned exterior from which hangs a bottle-green sign: Family Court.

Everywhere dogs: in the streets, standing in the dusty doorways, prowling, sleeping, yawning, snapping behind the barbed wire. And burning: sugar cane, garbage, the jungle. Smoke rises from behind the church at Westmoreland, from the yards of Hopewell, watched by ragged children on bicycles. There is always the fire and the dogs. Swooping down out of the mountains is a green promontory, a solid slug of foliage in the blue water. A sign, propped against the sea wall: 'Excited tours of corral reefs. Daily.'

And into the flat stretches the plain, russet coloured shacks, an isolated palm tree sways in the high wind. It looks like Vietnam; you can almost hear the choppers burst from the hillside. Otto is transfixed. The cyclist taps him on the shoulder, wants to start a conversation.

'Do you come here often?' he shouts.

'I don't know,' Otto answers.

And then we're onto a light brown road, winding up into the hills again. A child with a bright white bandage around his head sits on a cement post as we fly by. The sea slips behind the jungle. A quick pit stop at a roadside tin shack for a case of ice-cold Red Stripe beer. A yopa tree clicks overhead in a gust from the ocean wind, the driver snaps a bottle opener from his back pocket, snatches a beer and keeps driving. And then, as the van comes out of a tight turn and breaks into a shaded grove, he slams a tape into the deck. We riding along a ridge, the sea below us and the first reggae notes throb from the fleeing van:

The boys from Eglinton
Won't put down the Remington.
The youth of Eglinton
Won't put down the Remington.

The bass clumps and walks, hesitates, catches stride,

moves up the neck; the notes bubble in slow time, like melted chocolate on a slow boil. And with our white faces and skinny knees we stare out the window, speechless. Sure enough, soon there's the overpowering, sweet smell of ganja.

'The coolest, sweetest, easy-drawing rocket fuel in the whole world,' pronounces Otto. He holds a joint the size of a small baseball bat at arm's length, the smoke funnelling from his nose. He's like a helium balloon, this guy. I can almost see him float to the ceiling of the van and bounce lightly from beam to beam, like a brightly coloured child's toy. He hands it to me. I'm drunk and I'm getting crazy but not that crazy and I know this stuff will be too much, the one step too extended. It might bring on something really scary, not just paranoia but terror. This is not, one might say, the traditional beginning for a family vacation. Let's not think about kidnapping. Don't go inside. It's labyrinthine in there; you'll never get out. Better to stare blank-faced into the sun.

I have the joint in my hands. First get rid of it. Just holding it is scary. Like a stick of nitro on a bumpy road. I tap the cyclist on the shoulder and with a straight face, give it to him. He takes it; with my left eye I'm measuring him for a straitjacket. I can't help it. It feels darkly sadistic ... in a few seconds he'll think somebody let off a stun grenade in the middle of his head; he'll come unravelled like a ball of twine hurled across the floor. This ain't like getting high in the rec room and listening to Sgt. Pepper. This stuff will turn you inside out like a cucumber fish. He gives me the thumbs-up sign as he bears down on the joint. Like we're deep-sea divers squeezing into a bathysphere. I return the gesture. He can count on me, it says. I'll help peel him off the side of the van when the heel comes down. I promise.

More tiny chalk-white towns. School children in immaculate blue and brown uniforms march in leisurely groups along the side of the road. They shift only slightly, at the roar of the van. They call this a snowball, the day a new crop of whites roll wide-eyed from the airport through their town. They stand by the side of the road and watch as we whizz by, another carload ready for the slaughterhouse, children let loose at the circus – too much pink floss, too much cotton candy – they've seen a million vans streak out of the green hillside, those over-eager white faces peering out the windows like intelligent goldfish.

And then the heat. Sometimes we pull into a coast town. The town hall wavers like melting fudge, freezes in my memory and then we race down another green lane, into a meadow, another mile of high grass, another isolated palm tree, thirty feet high, bent double in the wind ...

The youth of Eglinton
Won't put down the Remington....

Huac, huac, huac.

I feel a slight weight press against my shoulder. In the midst of everything Fran has fallen asleep.

Chapter Six

I didn't know what it was that made people come apart
in Jamaica but I'd seen it happen a dozen times. They
came unravelled; they had bouts of tears in the grocery
store, tantrums in the post office. I remember coming
across a doctor from Minneapolis, fighting for the telephone at three in the morning. He'd woken up in a fit
of anxiety, convinced that something terrible was happening at home.

I don't know what it was but some mornings you
walked along that road by the sea and you thought of
things you hadn't thought about for years. It felt as if
you were going privately crazy. 'But this is my holiday,' you'd say, wiping away the tears after breakfast.
'I'm having fun.'

There was just something about the place; it took
you apart, that's for sure. But if you stayed long
enough, it put you back together.

Maybe it was the air; it was too thick, like pushing
through a wall of invisible balloons. It made you sleepy
just to breathe it. No wonder everything ambles here,

everything moves like syrup poured slowly from the can. Maybe it was the vegetation – too lush, too stridently green. Trees growing inside trees, the akee bulbs hanging red and bulbous like bull's balls. It was the heat, the sex, the grief, the loneliness that reached right from the cliff edges and grabbed you by the throat. It was the sound of a wheelbarrow in the yard, the bang of a nail hammered into a board, a yell from the road. It was the wild, uplifting surges of happiness, of optimism. It might be snatched away thirty yards from here, or tomorrow, or next month but for this second, as the Doctor's Wind blows the hot island air back out to sea, this moment is enough. It was the music, the reggae booming from fish huts and bars and from behind darkened, barred windows. A throbbing hallucinatory line of bass, throbbing like a toothache.

It was a peculiar darkness which came over you passing Cool Brown's, which caught you in mid-step and suddenly, inexplicably it was back, the sense that something was wrong, something neglected, something you should have done, should have looked after. A garden untended somewhere and disaster on the brink. And then, with the substance of mist, it evanesces as you turn the corner. It was the sense that something had been turned up inside you, that something you thought was dead was not.

'I'm going to town. Can I get you something?'

'Sure.'
'What do you want?'
'Anything.'

Night was falling when we arrived at the hotel. The sky was a dying orange.

La Mar was a small, white hotel in the cliffs, three miles up the road from town. A perfect jewel encrusted in the hillside. Franny and I were the last off the van. The driver wanted American money and I didn't have any. He held the Canadian twenty at arm's length as if it smelt bad, as if he wasn't sure what I'd done with it before I gave it to him. He turned it over and peered at it unhappily. My arm started to ache and I was no longer in a bartering mood.

'I can't take this,' he complained.

'You'll have to. It's all we have.'

He unwound the window and flagged down a passing bicyclist. A sweet, ragged old man agreed it wasn't American money but didn't know how much it was worth. He climbed back on his ancient Swinn and wobbled off.

'No,' the driver said, less convinced, 'I can't take this.'

'Come here tomorrow and I'll give it to you in American,' I said and opened the door. Franny slid off the seat and we moved up the stone walk. The van hesitated, honked its horn impotently and drove off.

We went into the hotel bar, a thatched, open-air affair with bamboo walls and a half-dozen red bullet tables. It was empty and quiet and that startled me. But I'd forgotten. This was off season. The west end of the town emptied out; even the Germans went home for a breather. There was no party waiting for us, no blasting speakers, no reggae versions of the Duke of Earl. Just an empty bar with a gleaming red floor. And a terrible sense of anticlimax. This wasn't what I'd remembered, what I'd come back for. I remembered it thronged with people, busy, electric, everybody up, everybody wanting, everybody sure they were going to get it. And now this – no music, the tables and chairs empty.

A yawning disappointment. I tried to resist it, push through it. I didn't want Franny to feel it. But had she? I wondered. I looked at her. She was bent down, scratching the back of her leg, her eyes staring at an object at the end of the room. It was the statue of a man and a woman, pressed together. It had been hacked out of rock-hard cedar by a long-departed guest.

No. She hadn't felt the sag. The island was still shiny and mysterious. That was it. The mystery was slipping out of the hotel for me. You could almost hear the back door shut. Where had everyone gone? All the people, the hats, the shirts in the airport, the van, Otto. They'd all left. They'd all gone somewhere else.

'Is there anyone here?'

Franny looked up at me. The door from the kitchen opened and an unsmiling young man with huge, sad eyes and a baseball hat stepped behind the bar. I didn't recognize him.

'Where is everyone? The place is like a morgue.'

'Do you want a room?' he replied calmly.

'Where's the owner? Harris? Where's Harris?'

'Do you want me to get him?'

'Yes. I'd like you to get him.'

'He's not here. He's in Kingston.'

'I'm thirsty,' Franny said. 'Where's J.?'

'Can we have a beer, please? A cold Red Stripe. And a pineapple juice for the child.'

'Apple juice.'

'No apple juice,' said the young man.

'How about orange juice?'

She thought for a minute.

'Orange juice,' she popped up, as if it were her idea.

'An orange juice, please.'

The bartender didn't reply. That annoyed me. I was sinking steadily into a black mood.

'Hello there? Did you hear me?'

The bartender turned and looked at me. I couldn't tell if he was smiling.

'What's your name?' I asked.

'Conway,' he said. 'My name is Conway.'

'Where's the boss?'

If the remark was meant to intimidate him, it didn't.

'So you want a room?'

'Yes. We'd like the room on the second floor. In the back. I can't remember the number.'

'Just a minute,' he said. 'I'll check,' and he disappeared into the kitchen. No beer, no orange juice. I'd only been in the country a few hours and already I had the fever. Sometimes, when you're in the mood, these fellows like Conway, they were enchanting, delightful; other times, it was like a room full of mosquitoes. You wanted to stuff every last bumbling, slow-talking nigger-skull into a vault and gas him.

But I had to put a lid on it. I didn't fly two thousand miles to snarl at the help.

Over the bar there was a sign.

It is my intention to apply for a spirit's licence at the next convening at Savanna-la-Mar in the county of Westmoreland.

When I was reading *Under the Volcano* – or, to be truthful, when I thought I was *in Under the Volcano* – I used to imbue that sign with a mystical significance. It didn't have any, of course. The sign had sat there through ten rainy seasons, white paint on black chip rock, not so much as a run in the letters.

'When *are* you going to get your liquor licence, Harris?' I used to ask him. He thought that was a gas.

'Any day now,' he'd say and we'd both be in stitches.

There was another sign over the entrance to both

residences, not so funny, although it never bothered me. It read: 'No Rastas, Prostitutes or Dreads on the hotel premises without strict permission from the management.' That turned off the freedom fighters, especially the white ones. There was a Kraut, I remember, who picked up his bags on the spot, refused to cross the threshold. He was an asshole and later that summer, he lost an eye in a brawl in Murphy's pool hall. With a black guy. Harris let him go. You couldn't make a twit like that understand it had nothing to do with religion. Harris didn't want his guests getting fleeced by a couple of beach niggers dressed up as holy men. And about the prostitutes, he didn't care. Just as long as they left when you did. And no snoozing while they cleaned out the neighbouring rooms.

You had to tie things down or they vanished. Big deal. That's just the way it was.

Franny whispered into my ear. 'Where is J.?' She made a funny little face. She was afraid of pestering me but she wanted to see her mother. In her way she was apologizing for being a nuisance.

In a while, Conway's head giraffed out of the kitchen door. 'One beer and one orange juice,' he said. He brought them around on a tray. 'Come,' he said, dead-pan.

We followed him out onto the patio and across the dark compound. It was lined with high bushes and trees, and a hammock sulked between two poles in the middle of the yard. Three dogs with mashed-up faces trailed behind us. Franny threw quick glances over her shoulder and squeezed closer to me until I nearly tripped over her.

We arrived at the main residence, a two-storey white-washed building poured from cement on the lip of the jungle, climbed up a dozen stairs in silence and stopped. From there you could see the ocean, milk-dappled in the starlight. Conway reached over his head and turned a light bulb. It flashed, covering the face of the building in a ghastly green hue. And then Franny jumped behind me.

'Look!' she whispered. In front of the door, illuminated by the eerie light, was a bundle of ruffled feathers lying in a pool of black ink. It had neither head nor tail. Gingerly, Conway extended a long, running-shoed foot and flipped it over.

'They're very stupid birds,' he said. 'They think they can fly through glass.'

He picked it up by a limp wing; there was a spatter of dime-sized blood drops on the cement and he hurled the bird into the jungle. It landed with a rustle. As he started to speak there was another sound, this time of paws over leaves as the dogs picked up the scent of the dead meat.

'How often does that happen?' I asked.

'Yes,' he replied.

Conway turned a giant key in the lock. The door

swung open and he clicked on the overhead light. The white box of a room was washed in a light as dazzling as a North African afternoon.

Franny squinted and peered about hopefully. No J.

'It's very bright in here,' I said, to say something.

There were two sheet-covered beds and two windows with pink orlon curtains; they looked synthetic and silly, but you could hear the ocean.

'How long are you staying?' Conway asked, standing by the door.

'I don't know.'

'It's 130 dollars U.S. a week.'

'I'll talk to the boss about it.'

He hesitated.

'It's okay, you know. I've been here before.'

He was about to pull the door behind him when I added hurriedly, 'I'm coming down later for a drink. You'll still be open, won't you?' He nodded. Franny shot me a quick frightened glance.

Conway shut the door finally and left us, Franny and me, sitting on separate beds, still squinting in the stunning light.

'Pretty bright in here, isn't it Fran?'

She didn't answer and I knew what she was thinking.

'Are you going down to the bar?' she asked.

'Yes, I am. In a little while when you're asleep.'

'Why are you going down to the bar?'

'I want to have a drink.'

'Why don't you go down to the bar and get the drink and bring it back here and drink it?'

'I want to go down to the bar for a while.'

'I just hope they don't smash the glass.'

'Who, Fran? Who's going to smash the glass?'

'The birds,' she said plaintively; her eyes glistened. Hadn't I said J. was going to be here? Where was she? Did her plane crash? She was working herself up and up. In a moment she'd be in hysterics. A small animal in uncomprehending fright.

She sat on the bed with her teddy in her arm and stared miserably at the floor. She swung her legs to and fro. I was starting to feel sick. My arm hurt again. I was afraid of fainting. Something had to be done quickly. I wanted to tell her that I'd hoped things would be different. I'd wanted her not to miss her mother, at least not so much, so soon. But nothing was working. It was slipping into her blond head that I was lying to her. Tomorrow it would be worse. There'd be more questions, more vague answers, more chirpy, unconvincing efforts to change the subject, more looks of suspicion from her and sooner or later it'd come out and I already imagined her screaming, scarlet-faced, in a crowded restaurant, 'I'm not supposed to be here! You stole me and I want to go home!'

I couldn't stand her unhappiness. The strain was making my hands shake. We sat under a white overhead light without exchanging a word, no movement except for her legs swinging and the whole nightmarish episode played itself in my imagination. I was on the verge of a confession.

'You know what's happened don't you Fran?'

She said nothing.

'She missed her plane.'

'I don't think she's coming. She never misses her plane.'

I waited a moment. 'I'm going to stay with you until you're asleep and then I'm going to phone her. Then we'll know when she's coming.'

'Can I speak to her?'

'No. You'll be asleep.' I thought she might start crying. 'There's no phone here. The phone's a long way from here. I'll wake you up after I call. I promise, Franny.'

'Is she coming tomorrow?'

'I don't think tomorrow.' I moved closer to her. 'Look at me.'

I stroked her hair. 'Get into bed and I'll rub your back. Soon you'll see J.'

She said nothing.

'I promise. Now into bed. We'll have a story.'

'I want to hear the story about J. arriving in the morning.'

She took off her jeans, her green alligator T-shirt, folded them neatly on a chair and scampered into bed.

She pulled the yellow flowered sheet to her bottom lip.

'How about *Madelaine and the Bad Hat*?' I suggested.

At that moment there was a rattle outside the room. Someone was standing on the other side of the door and there was a brushing sound. Conway stood expressionless with a dust bin and a broom. 'I think you'd have more luck with a mop,' I said, but he continued to sweep. I took a candle from the dresser, set it on the floor beside her bed, lit it and turned off the overhead light. Pulled the curtain. Outside the deathly green hue, the thick salt air. A door being shut and hurriedly locked, an impatient voice I partially recognized....

Franny and I sat in the candlelit room, while outside heavy, bottle-neck flies whirled and clicked and thudded against the glass light bulb. There was a high-pitched, almost inaudible, hum of electricity in the wires.

And then from the bar, reggae music, the words indistinguishable, the bass line tickled across the yard like a mouse starting and stopping along a floorboard.

We listened carefully in the dark:

Puff she puff no bother puff
pon Rasta
Tough she tough no bother tough
pon Rasta.

'Do you understand what the brown people say?'

'Not much,' I said. 'Is your bed comfortable?'

'Hot. I'm boiling. I've got bites.'

She lay on her stomach, her face pressed sideways against the mattress. Honey-dewed features.

'I got stuck in the bathroom today at school. I had to go out under the door.'

'Like smoke?'

'No. Like a newspaper.'

I rubbed the back of her neck.

'No. My back. The tickly part. And tell me about J. and the airplane.'

'There are other things here, you know Fran, other than your mom.'

'My mom is more exciting. To me.'

'What does she look like? I mean right now?'

'Long hair and she wears T-shirts.'

She wriggled impatiently.

'When she comes,' I began, 'it'll be after your nap....'

'Start in the morning,' she interrupted.

'We'll get up and have a glass of orange juice just across the road and then we'll put on shorts and a hat and we'll walk up the road and go swimming....'

'Will there be fish?'

'Yes.'

'Red ones? Blue ones? Pink ones?'

'All colours.'

'Do they bite?'

'No. They're little, the size of your hand.'

'But they don't bite.'

'No. They press against your legs when you walk in the water.'

'Like flowers?'

'Like black-eyed Susans in a field.'

From the bar the bass line changed. It was leisurely, a Sunday stroll up the guitar neck.

'And then, after the swim, we put our towels on the balcony railing to dry. We flag down a taxi and go to town. We buy a slice of watermelon. And a black coral ring for you. And some coco bread. We put everything on the bed to show J. And you'll get under the sheets, like you're doing now, and we'll talk about everything we did and then, when you think you're asleep and dreaming, you'll hear something and you'll still think you're dreaming, and you'll hear your name and you'll open both eyes and look up and who'll be there?'

There was no answer.

I pulled up the sheet. I listened to her breathing. I watched her back rise and fall in the candlelight. I blew out the flame and slipped to the door.

'I'll see you in the morning Franny.' But she didn't answer.

Chapter Seven

'Overproof,' I said when I got back to the bar. Conway poured a shot; it sat sullen in the glass, clear and oily. He asked if I wanted it with ice, a 'steel bottom.'

'No. Just a water chaser. I can't sip it.'

He poured himself a shot and mixed it with goat's milk.

'Do you want a tab?'

'Sure. Put your drink on it too.'

He opened a yellow notebook and made a meticulous entry.

I stared at the O.P., bracing myself. Then like a high diver when the moment arrives I took a concentrated breath, put the glass to my lips, closed my eyes, threw it back, waited a beat, then swallowed.

The taste came, that horrible staleness as if it had been festering under the dock for three hundred years. There was no nausea, just an involuntary shudder like snapping a towel fresh from the dryer. Dexter was right. This stuff was for preserving frogs. I dumped a glass of water into the hold after it.

I wiped the tears from my eyes and replaced the glass carefully on the bar.

'Another, please.'

But Conway had a little surprise for me first. He poured a shot onto the polished surface of the bar. 'Now watch this,' he said, lighting a match. He touched the flame to the liquid and the puddle popped into a blue flame. Christmas time. Plum pudding. A dozen turkey-gobbling faces jump back in surprise and laughter.

Merry Christmas!

'That's what you're putting in your stomach,' he said.

We both watched the flame thoughtfully. I sipped my beer. It had gone warm. You have to drink the beer fast here. It's got a life expectancy of five minutes. After that it's warm and cloying and backs up in your throat.

I wandered over to the table.

'Do you want music?' he asked.

'Sure.'

'What?'

'Anything. But let me have a beer first.'

He went over to a small wooden cubicle in the corner of the bar, opened it with a key and began to shuffle through a ragged stack of record albums.

'Last year, a guy came in here,' he started, 'and tried

to buy a bottle of overproof. Mr. Sam didn't sell him one. The guy was drunk; he couldn't speak. He went down the road and got one at Brown's. They sold him one. They don't care. So he walked down the road to town, drinking the overproof straight from the bottle. Somebody make him a bet at the Wharf Club that he can't drink the rest of it in one swallow. So he tried and he fall right onto the floor and can't get up. An ambulance come all the way from Sav, but he's dead already.'

After a suitable pause, I changed the subject.

'What record are you going to play?'

'Just wait and see.'

'Play something good, okay? Something up.'

' "Night Nurse"? You like that? Your friend Dexter, he loves that song. I hear him coming up the road late at night. He sounds like a frog. He comes up the road croaking like a big frog and he's singing "Night Nurse." '

'I want to find him tomorrow.'

'He's in Redground. He doesn't come here anymore. Him and Mr. Sam had a fight about money. But you'll hear him. Tonight. Croaking up the road like a frog.'

'The guy in the Wharf Club,' I started. 'What did he die of?'

'His brain exploded.'

'A brain hemorrhage?'

'A brain hemorrhage.'

His brain exploded. I repeated the words softly and looked out the window. A brain hemorrhage. Like the one I was having now. I was getting off and getting off big. This wasn't a drunk; this was a state of anaesthesia, a numbing of the face, a gentle tug of release. Getting off and getting off big. God, don't let me touch the ground until I'm sound asleep and winter's over.

Conway eased into the booth opposite me. The conversation meandered tipsily around the island, the rumour of Cuban guns, a machete death at Black Springs. A teenage black boy had been hacked to death for stealing a camera from an American villa. They carried off the pieces and let the word out as a warning. There were no charges laid. More idle chat – about rape, plastic cups on the beach and on and on and on. And then we came back to the overproof like the leit-motif of the evening. We were both in the can now, both floating pleasantly downstream.

'You know Conway,' I said. 'There's a saying that if you've got the patience to sit by the river, eventually you'll see the bodies of all your enemies float by.'

Without comment, he went behind the bar and poured a double. I focussed hard on the glass and sat up straight, trying to psyche my stomach into neutrality. This time there was no taste, no burn. The O.P. ran down thick and soundless, landing with the clean whack of a lacrosse stick – it kept coming back at you in waves. I could feel my bowels turning to water. I took off my glasses and wiped them on my sleeve. It looked as if I was having a quiet, after-dinner weep.

Gradually, after a while, the bar appeared to be filling up with people, and I had the feeling, a premonition almost, that I was in on the very early stages of a splendid party, when the cars pull up after sunset and the guests spill out. There was an amiable early-evening buzz of excitement: suntans and clear eyes, freshly showered hair and white cotton shirts. Indeed I had the sensation of knowing everyone, of being in the bosom of good friends.

I sat beside an arched window and imagined the evening as it unfolded its magic. Outside, in the spotlight from the street lamps, there were figures, white and black, silent, passing up and down like river vessels. White dresses, German accents, a pair of bicycles, a bobbing flashlight, high cheekbones and straight blond hair. There were groups of blacks, trousered with bright synthetic shirts. They walked faster, in bigger groups, the island patois lilting, falling behind them like lilac petals. They headed down the road to the Soon Come, the Wharf Club. In the warm, salt-drenched air they passed quickly, framed by the windows.

The wind blew in from the sea, through the palm trees, the khaki button trees, the sea grape; it blew through the arched windows and brushed my face like a lime-scented handkerchief. Veiled in a gauze cocoon I stared straight ahead. And waited.

And in a while the O.P. clicked in another notch. I moved ahead, stepping into pockets of still, warm air. I yawned abruptly and stretched. The suddenness of the action surprised me. Terror gone, fear gone, loneliness gone, J. gone. J. gone. Like a limb that's been amputated, it aches dully, inescapably. A bullet, dispatched soundlessly thousands of miles away, arrives, not with a whistle through the grass, not with a violet mushroom explosion but like the expanding rings of an abscess, one thought bleeding into another, one moment overlapping into the other until both pulse blood-red with her absence. Simply put, she is gone.

This month, it is the beginning of the rainy season and the wind starts way out to sea, a hundred times further out than Uriah's boat and bobbing gas lamp.

On those grey days the wind rushes up the beach so ferociously it can cupcake the thatched roof of a house, smack you across the cheek with your shirt, snap the glasses off your face and send them running along the sand like an exotic two-legged crab.

I sit near the seawall in Jamaica and I hear the intimate bass tones of a passing couple, arm in arm. Their voices edge towards you, rising from the dark road, dark silhouettes cloaked in privacy. There are other voices, full of innuendo. They draw your attention in bits like shavings seduced towards a magnet ... as if your heart will break at the mention of her, as if you will fall forever out of sound and human touch.

The voices are insistent, a phantom limb that throbs in the early morning hours when you rub a knee which isn't there, cradle an arm which is gone ... she is gone. Thin voices, old conversations, minor triumphs, a gash of cruelty hurled between us like a machete, they spin around and around and come out like stale cartoons.

Gone for good? Hard to imagine a room without J. in it, a day without the phone ringing or the door pushed open and her there. But it was over and done and one day, six months after the fact, I knew it. It was six o'clock in the morning and I was reading, smoking a cigarette. I got out of bed, went into the bathroom and splashed cold water on my face. When I looked in the mirror I knew she was gone and it was for keeps. My reflection gleamed back at me and I had a terrible staleness in my mouth.

Over, as simple as that? Impossible.

And then I started dreaming about her – odd after so many years of dreaming about everything but her, the postman, the baker, the candlestick maker, odd to start only after she was gone ... perfect though, the kind of joke J. would like.

Sometimes it might be the lingering scent of a woman's perfume in the subway that makes me feel I'll never get her back. Why sometimes, just the idea that she's gone whips me to my feet and pushes me around the room with a stupid, frightened smile on my face. I fall into a bar like a hot kid into an August pond. Dead drunk, floundering like a big moon-eyed bass, I find myself rehearsing little speeches, minor speeches, things I might whisper to make her laugh, to make her soft like before, whispered fragments in the dark, if only she were listening....

Sometimes I wonder if I haven't left it all a bit too late, if I haven't waited until she was truly gone before I let myself fall in love with her.

Two strips of starched linen stepped off the road, flickered against the black grating and moved exuberantly into the bar. The girls wore matching Yale sweatshirts and recently purchased linen pants, tied at the waist. 'We're from Minneapolis,' one said, addressing the room. 'Good girls go to heaven,' the other giggled, 'bad girls go everywhere.'

It was obviously a joke they'd been enjoying all evening and which improved with repetition.

They were joined presently by two boys, both American and handsome in an American way. They engaged the girls in a flip badinage, eight brown arms resting on the bar, raised in emphasis or laughter.

I watched them with fascination. Two boys and two girls. It looked like such fun they were having, such fun; they illuminated the crowded, smoky bar; it was as if they had drawn the spotlight onto themselves while around them, in blue shadows, the others purred happily. I breathed a sigh of envy. Everyone had time, heaps and heaps of time. It looked so delicious, those sweet, early moments between boys and girls. The bar crackled with friendly, happy chat.

A game of backgammon, a short, choppy dance step, a bridge game, dark rum and the smell of Jamaican coffee. Two Chinese lanterns hung from the ceiling: red, corrugated globes like gigantic drops of blood. The aroma physical, suggestive, anticipatory: salt and sun on fresh bodies. Under the soft Chinese lanterns she brushes his arm with a lingering glance like the last ray of sunlight when the day is dying.

How nice to meet J. all over again, to slip up beside her in a bar like this, on an island like this. 'I was hoping you'd be here. Can I buy you a beer? I haven't done this for ages.'

'Me neither.'

Just stand at the bar, looking great, the whole night and the whole island ahead of you, stand at the bar, listen to the music and have a great time. We've paid our toxic, domestic dues. This is the payoff. Touching elbows at the bar, to chat about nothing at all. Sweet and funny and full of personality. How sweet. How ... overdue.

Somewhere in this bar, I hear the scratch of an old

record and Edith Piaf sings 'La Vie en Rose.' It makes me very sentimental and for a moment I'm sure that J. is coming to the island for a reunion. I'm quietly, modestly convinced. I run over in my mind the places I'll show her; imagine a little mid-morning outing to Bloody Bay, six miles past the lighthouse into the cliffs. We'll have a picnic, Fran, her mother and I. We're getting back together and I want it to go well.

At night we'd have dinners by the water at Blue Cave. After the child had gone to bed. There'd be time for just the two of us. There was a great deal to say and now there would be time for everything.

Things would come out right. There'd be no awkwardness, no explanations. The words would be right, nothing omitted, nothing ... hurtful. It would all make sense, this time; we were together and then we were apart and then we're together again. Painful sometimes but for the best because ... because we're here, now, together. Now there'll be time. 'What were you thinking that day on the street? Was it that? I thought it might be that. I hoped it might be that.'

A courtship. We would have a second courtship and fall in love again, properly.

'I had a dream about you, you know. I did. I dreamt I saw you stepping from a sailboat. You carried a basket. I don't know what was inside.'

'Odd to have got it so wrong J., so incredibly wrong.'

Getting back together. But what if she came here, what if she came and didn't want me anymore? I'd be forced to watch as she discovered with each passing day in Eden how out of love she'd fallen. Lying in bed together, under a splash of equatorial stars, waiting for her knee to touch mine. The dogs bark, the fires burn, the roosters crow and I lie beside her with a sinking stomach. Paralysed, the two of us. Covering her mouth with embarrassment, she might say, 'Oh dear.' And who will turn over first? Who's giving up first? In the morning she gets up too quickly, dresses in the bathroom, asks brightly if you know a good place for breakfast. All day long, in the walk from the cliffs to town we blame the heat. 'You can't think in this heat. It's impossible to even talk.'

Too many drinks before dinner, two oblong plates topped with untouched lobster.

'Don't sulk,' she says.

'I wish you'd stop punishing me.'

'I'm not punishing you. I've just stopped loving you.'

Rum loosens the tongue.

'What a lovely thing to say, blah, blah, blah.'

I surfaced. I felt as if I were tearing myself away from a raging party, shouted goodbyes and apologies over a din of music and bright, animated conversation.

The bar was empty. The ashtrays were empty. The

polished red floor was empty. The rip in my arm pulsed comfortably. Conway teetered on the edge of his stool in the record cubicle. He was watching me. I must have been speaking out loud. He went back to shuffling through a handful of 45s.

Chapter Eight

I woke up deathly sick God knows how many hours later. I thought I had the plague. At first I couldn't remember where I was and I didn't care. I just wanted to go back to sleep, to drift back down in an aquarium coma and lurk at the bottom, hidden in the cool muck. Somewhere to hide, somewhere the memories of the last twenty-four hours couldn't get me. They could bump their heads against the plate glass of my tank. They could press their snouts against the windows. They could peer at me with foolish eyes ... they could watch but they could not come in.

Horripilating. Big word. Big hangover. Dogs barked; the moon yelled. In the fluttering green someone hummed 'Hello Dolly' into a telephone. The world was up for sale. Make your offer and stand back.

Gradually the whole mess came back to me and I threaded my way back through the evening and the afternoon like a blind man. Each image hovered into focus – brimming with sensation – a blood stain on a snow-white blotter, growing in larger and larger circles. Everything else thick and motionless like awaking under water with nothing but the occasional sigh from a rusted waterpipe. Next to me, I could make out the figure of a small child. I crossed the floor and bent over Franny's bed. She'd tossed off her sheet and lay uncovered on her back, her face to one side with a brown teddy bear snuggled into her arm. Beads of perspiration dotted her forehead and upper lip.

I opened the door and looked out onto the backyard. Twenty yards away, across the scraggly yard, four mah-jongg players sat in silent concentration. I heard the click of the ivory men as they slid across the board into new defences. North Wind, South Wind, Dragon. To their right a large yellow dart board glared across the compound like an angry dandelion. It was illuminated by a circle of Christmas bulbs.

Faint music. I could not remember leaving the bar. Or why. A quarrel? Tears? I had the sense of having been seduced into long painful confessions. But by whom?

Sleep was impossible; my hands were shaking. I'd fallen asleep with my clothes on and I stank of sour anxious sweat.

I sat on the side of the bed and tried to cry. My tear ducts must have been dehydrated from the overproof. I managed a few squeaks but I couldn't get the tears rolling. I thought about the bad things I'd done to nice people but that didn't work either. I felt too sorry for myself to fuss about them.

Everything was coming unstuck and tomorrow ... just the thought of tomorrow made me dart into the bathroom to brush my teeth.

But really now, how could I have gotten so plastered in the face of such a crisis? But if I hadn't gotten drunk, maybe I wouldn't have pulled this caper in the first place. And that business about a reunion. That wasn't just drunk; that was loony. I scrambled through my memory, hoping to God I hadn't unburdened myself of that one in public. But no, I'd been alone. It was a private moment, a crazed vector that no one had to know about.

Hardly a reunion.

Before long I was going in circles, pacing the room. One minute I saw myself as a martyr, the next as the lowliest of cretins. I blamed it on the hangover. It was tearing chunks out of me. A monster like this one doesn't go away by lunch. Sometimes they don't hit their stride until mid-evening the next day. By then I'd be cringing in a basket in the hotel basement.

The rest of the night was going to be agony, unless I did something. There was no alternative. In for a penny, in for a pound. I'd have to hot foot my way to Cool Brown's and buy a couple of downers. Nothing serious, just a couple of valium. It wouldn't kill the hangover but it might take it down a few registers, stop the knife twisting in the wound, so to speak. Like the man said, once you're on the conveyor belt, it's a son of a bitch to get off.

Just anticipating made me feel better. Two round ten-milligram valium washed down with an ice-cold beer and I'd be back on my feet. Perhaps not in racing form but at least not paralysed, at least not the slope-shouldered whore I glimpsed peeking back at me in the mirror.

A beer, a couple of pills and I'd be back here in fifteen minutes. I'd be okay. And I could clear up this mess with the child and her mother, take a new tack.

But get well first.

I pulled the sheet up over Franny's shoulder, turned out the light, walking briskly across the yard, stuffing my hands in my pockets in a posture of nonchalance. The mah-jongg players looked up as I passed the table. I heard one of them say, 'There are no snakes on the island.' Why, I'm not sure, but the words shocked me as if I'd stuck a knife in the toaster. Were they talking to me, making fun of me? I snapped my head around. Seeing me stiffen, a mustached young man smiled apologetically. 'It's true,' he offered meekly, 'there *are* no poisonous snakes on the island.'

I edged towards the shadows, frightened they might see on my face how crazy I thought I looked. I expected laughter, even names hurled after me. But nothing came. At the front of the hotel a German couple sat reading fashion magazines. They observed my passage with glassy eyes and a nod of numb acknowledgement. I looked again. The fear of running into someone I knew had taken a twist in my imagination, with the result that everyone seemed familiar, as if, in the course of an energized evening, we'd spent hours together, engrossed in a conversation around someone's kitchen table. A conversation which I now, with characteristic shallowness, was unable to recall.

Cool Brown was an irascible, unsmiling old porcupine. He didn't like anyone. He ran a rickety bike-rental joint a mile down the road from the hotel. His machines were a wreck, salt rusted, spokes missing, gears that slipped and castrated you on the crossbar. But he had other sidelines which he operated from his bamboo shack; he rented masks, snorkels; he sold soiled postcards, beer, Pepsi and orange fizz. He also sold downers, all kinds of downers, mandrax, tuinals, seconals, valium, phenobarbital. He moved a little speed too, low-grade stuff, usually blood-red diet capsules which his brother, Elton, boosted from a pharmacy warehouse in Kingston. Brown had six kids; they were nice kids, full of tickles and quick smiles. They had spindly little arms as strong as cast iron and they played dominoes. They ran the place. In the afternoons you'd find Brown taking the shade in a hammock beside the ice cooler, his flat, predatory face coal-black under a baseball cap. Some people thought he was colourful, eccentric, a real 'local character.' I thought he was an asshole. But I treated him with respect, even obsequiousness. That made him despise me.

At all costs, I didn't want to come slinking down the

road one morning with a two-hundred-pound hang-over an inch over my head and discover the old goat had cut me off. No sir. When I ran that scenario by, it was no trouble to pop a cheerful 'Morning Brown' from my lips; no trouble to tip my hat and give the kids a pat on the head.

'Top of the morning to you Brown. Say, got any reds?'

It was a ten-minute walk along the cliff road to Brown's, and I was as jumpy as a hamster. Everything spooked me, the wind in the trees, a dog snarling in the jungle, the moon passing behind a cloud. It all struck me as ominous, a warning. As I rounded the last corner I was thrilled to see Cool Brown's garish yellow sign lit up. I was so relieved that for a second I fancied I liked him. What a great old guy, open at this time of night, a real regular guy – a hard-working gent – and a parent to boot.

It was shit of course. The moment I had the downers in my mouth I'd go back to loathing him again. From the dark road I heard the pistol retort of the dominoes slapped against the board.

The whole family was up. Brown lurked in the sha-dows, smoking a cigarette.

'Evening Brown.'

He looked at me.

'How's business?'

'Cool.'

'That's good.'

'Like the sign say. Everything cool here.'

'Good. Got any bombers?'

'Mandrax.'

'How much?'

'Five U.S.'

'A bit high, no?'

'No.'

'How long you had them?'

'Fresh today.'

'Too much. How about valium?'

'Got seconal.'

'No. I want to drink too.'

'Valium then. A dollar each.'

'They're fresh too, Brown?'

'Today.'

'A regular farmer's market here, Brown.'

'How many?' he asked.

'Ten.'

He stuck a black paw into a waist-high wicker basket and pulled out a dark, foot-tall bottle. Expertly he shook out ten.

'Have you got anything to put them in?' I asked.

'No.'

'Let me have some foil from your cigarettes then.'

He sighed. This was a bother. I laid down twenty dollars Jamaican, stacked the pills into two piles, folded over the foil, gave it a twist and dropped it into my pocket.

'Thanks Brown. Nice to see you again.' He'd already shuffled into the back. We'd skip the handshake.

It was after one in the morning. I smiled at his kids – I felt better already – and stepped light-footedly back onto the road. I'd have a beer and a drambuie at Pee Wee's, drop a couple of valium and then, when the slow mushroom stirred and I relaxed a little, I'd get on the blower. Clear this business up. But first, I'd get back to Franny.

The road was dark. I came abreast of Uriah's shack. A coal lamp burned in the glassless window, illuminated a child's multi-coloured drawing of 'magic mushrooms.' There was a boxnet on the grass in front of the fire, a tethered goat, a rusted slinky hanging from a Christmas bulb, the smell of barracuda and dull, burnished metal pots ... the shack leaned drunkenly to the side. His wife Jennie hadn't seen me. She sat by the fire, looking down the road, large features, smooth-skinned, her head bandana'd in a red handkerchief. Uriah lay asleep in a hammock with two small children sleeping like spoons on his stomach. In the background a radio crackled with static and an overseas voice with a British accent announced the week's cricket scores. For a second I wanted to cross the road. You could see the ocean from here and I lingered. The trees parted, the rocks rose sharp and dramatic and then the ocean crashed and the moon lay like a streak of white light across the water.

Nothing moved in Uriah's portrait. The embers were dying. The wind tugged gently at me and I moved on.

Above me, those peculiar, leafless branches. They grew long, wooden shapes, three feet long, curved like Chinese bows. They rattled when you shook them and children loved them for toys. But tonight, they looked ominous and frightening; you could almost hear the brush of a buzzard's wing: John Crow, always circling. I'd seen him earlier, high floating, circling above the green sea, running along the lip of the jungle.

A dog snarled in the bush then hurled himself against the chicken wire fence; it bent like a spider web. I froze, frightened that he'd break through the mesh. Ugly, snout-scarred mongrels, there were hundreds of them, guarding each tiny plot of land between here and town.

I'd forgotten. From this point on I'd need a stick. Sometimes in the frenzy of a pack, they'd spill onto the road, back you against a tree and really scare the hell out of you. They were cowardly little monsters. Their blood boiled when they smelt fear. The rest of the time they were jackals, chewing on chicken bones and old cans from piles of smoking garbage.

I foraged around in the bushes until I came up with a good staff, a good strong one, four feet long with a dead weight at the end; something I could knock a mutt into the next county with. And then I saw him.

Dexter Alexander: liar, racist, part-time money changer, vendor of motorcycle parts, Scottish terrier and king-size juicer. He ran at a feverish pitch of energy and sometimes, unless you could match it or you were a woman he wanted, he made people feel pushed around. He didn't talk, he sort of barked at you but he could be exquisitely, irreverently funny and great company and it felt, initially anyway, like a godsend to run into him, just the wild, uplifting tonic I needed.

He stood in the twinkling light of the Town Talk bar, threw back his head and drained the last drop of beer from a bottle. He'd picked up on me, although he hadn't seen me yet. He swung his large head in a slow circle, antennae twitching in the night air. He caught sight of me and ran down the bank in quick short steps, arriving breathless at my feet. He was red faced, tanned as a nut, his red hair curling furiously, yet even as he stood in front of me, something sagged and I couldn't help but feel a twinge of disappointment. And I also knew instantly that I couldn't tell him about Franny. Dexter was notoriously loose lipped but that wasn't the only problem.

What I had forgotten and now remembered was

that Dexter, in addition to being a great Caribbean 'character' was a peculiarly envious man. Sometimes as a way of getting even he told outright lies about his friends or betrayed their confidences. It was an unfortunate quality that you chose to ignore if you wanted to like him. And I did, a lot, but I knew better than to trust him. But it was there, this small, pusillanimous streak that cut right through to his heart and when he tumbled down from the hilltop, the last piece of the Jamaican puzzle fell into place. Abruptly, on all fronts, I realized what an unmitigated disaster I'd landed Franny and me in.

'Wait,' is all he said and he hurled his bottle into the jungle. In a second he'd pulled his sweatshirt over his head and hurled it contemptuously after the bottle. A cyclist rolled by unsteadily. 'I've been fighting with nigger whores over money. My landlady! I hate those nigger whores, don't you Junior?' He yelled after the retreating cyclist. He threw open his arms. 'Imagine, fighting in the street! Me? He attacked me. All those niggers standing around, watching. Christ! I hate those nigger whores!'

I wanted desperately to like him, to have an ally, but he grated on me and I wanted to flee. But I had nowhere to go except that excruciating white room and the sleeping child.

J. had met Dexter once. He showed up one afternoon looking for me at the film festival. To this day she makes a gesture of plugging her nose whenever his name comes up. I thought maybe a drink might help. Dexter used to say about women: 'Sometimes you can drink 'em pretty' and that's what I did for the rest of the night: whenever I came up against something I didn't like, I just threw back another drink and waited to feel different. So we marched back up the hill and had a quick round of Appelton's dark, straight up, no ice, no water. Its effect was an immediate calming. I had another. It wasn't too long before I was feeling almost okay about where I was and then I started to like Dexter again.

'Say,' he said, rushing to fill the silence, 'do you remember that little Jew from Illinois – Champaign, Illinois? The one with the tits? She screwed half the Krauts in town right under my window. I thought she had a trampoline down there.'

'Sure,' I said, warming to the rum. 'I saw her today. In the van. The girl with the tapedecks?'

'I'm gonna fuck her,' he said. 'I swear to God this year I'm gonna do it. She's been hanging around me like a puppy. What's with her?'

'Dexter,' I began, 'I can't stay.'

'I almost got her last year, the night Yellow Man was in town, but she ended up with that prick from Ibiza. Anyway he dumped her. He didn't give a hoot and she found that out.'

He took a drag off his cigarette, sucking it down to

his boot laces, blew it out like he wanted it to reach the moon.

'What's with her?' he asked almost angrily.

'I don't know Dexter. I just arrived.'

'Well then have a cigarette. Here. I'll light the goddamn thing for you.'

'I got your note,' I said.

'What note?'

'The note you left in my apartment.'

'Of course I remember the note! I remember everything. That's the difference between you and me. No matter how pissed I get I remember every last bloody detail! So let's go have a peek at Tiger Bates' mom. She just died. It's an open coffin.'

'Gee, Dexter,' I said, 'I don't know if I want to go to a funeral my first night in town.'

'It's not a funeral. The funeral was last Thursday. This is a wake – and a hell of a wake at that. It's in its fifth day.'

'I've got to get back to the hotel. I'm travelling with my daughter.'

'Oh yeah,' he said, scrutinizing me. When Dexter scrutinized you, he moved his face close – too close, some thought – and bounced his eyes around your face as if looking for the flaw. It could be very disconcerting, particularly if you hated your latest haircut or suspected yourself of a weak chin.

'Yeah,' I said and to my surprise averted my eyes.

I'm sure he noticed but fortunately Dexter had seldom more than a fleeting interest in other people's difficulties.

'Well fuck the kid,' he said and laughed.

'No, really, I have to get back. It's her first day.'

He cut me off. 'It's my first day too.' A pause then he added cagily: 'Is she waiting up for you or what?'

'No, she's asleep.'

'So what are you going to do? Go back and watch her sleep?'

'...'

'A lovely picture that,' he sniffed.

'Listen,' I said, 'I'll walk you back to the hotel. Come and have a vodka with me.'

'I hate walking. I don't come to Jamaica to walk. I'll drive you. Anyway I got to stop and see somebody near your hotel. Business. I won't be long. I left it so damn late now. And I got to use the phones at the Beach Club too, that is if the niggers haven't stolen the earpieces.'

'Drop me off at the hotel,' I said.

'I can't believe you don't remember that girl,' he rattled on. 'She sat around Xtabi spreading that olive oil all over her tits.' He chuckled unpleasantly. 'What a farce. Everybody walking around with a banana in their pants pretending not to notice. And don't think she didn't know what was going on, am I right?' He nodded his head emphatically.

'Dexter, I've got a tremendous hangover.'

'So have a drink. If you feel shitty have a drink. Always works. You know the other night I had a dream. I dreamt I ran out of money and I had to swim all the way home.'

A twist of wind burst around the shack, whisking the ember clean off the end of his cigarette. He looked at the dead butt calmly. 'I hate the wind,' he said. 'Never could understand what it was good for.'

Dexter disappeared behind the building and cranked up his motorcycle. The headlamp flashed on and the engine revved. The next second we pushed out onto the road. That was the beginning of it. There was a point, just as we passed the hotel, when I could have stopped, could have gotten off. I could have said stop, and I did but not loud enough and Dexter didn't hear me over the engine. I let the hotel slip by and then I let myself float and I didn't wake up until the light broke in an orange bar between the khaki trees and it was morning.

I just let it go and said fuck it. I let it go because I thought she was asleep and it'd be okay. I let it go because Dexter always sounded as if great things happened to him and I'd had just enough to drink to believe it. I let it slip by because I didn't want to sit in a whitewashed room and watch a child sleep. I let it go because I couldn't stand the idea of my own company. I wanted a piece of Dexter's irreverence. I stayed out, and this is the kicker, because I'd already fucked up bad and I didn't think I could make it any worse.

The road was grey, pock-marked with broken asphalt, and we were going too fast. It was dangerous running like this. You could fly off the road, careen into the sea, but it made me less frightened about the other things, the room back at the hotel and what I was going to do when I got back there. That's the great thing about scaring the shit out of yourself on a motorcycle. You can only be scared of one thing at a time.

Somewhere, five minutes past the silk-worm lights of the hotel, we slowed abruptly, stretched at the end of a long elastic band. The gravity pulled us forward and we turned right into the hills, bumping up a potholed road. The moon broke loose from the clouds and we lurched to a halt in a moon-soaked field. Across the way sat a strawberry wedge of a house. We're off the bike and Dexter is calling across the field, calling out a name I don't know. There's no answer to Dexter's call, no answer from the strawberry house; his voice is blown across the field, back out to sea.

Such a beautiful night, the air so maddeningly soft I wanted to weep. It felt as if I had fallen down the longest flight of stairs in the world and landed at the bottom. I looked up to see a sky that seemed as if someone had overturned a huge black bowl over the world and dressed it in pulsing lights. In the almost holy stillness, even Dexter was silent, and I heard my heart thumping in my chest, and there was a lump in my throat. If only

J. could see me now, in this field, not even she could have the cruelty not to take me back again.

I wanted desperately to tell Dexter about Franny and while I rehearsed the words in my head, a terrible sense of dread came over me, and then a sense of loss, of mourning. Dexter said something but I didn't answer. I was following a black funeral procession up a hill and in the hearse was a child's coffin. The black line of limousines slowly wound its way through the mud and snow to the top of the bald hill where impatient men with shovels smoked cigarettes and waited for the sermon to be finished. Ashes to ashes, dust to dust. For what we are about to receive may the lord make us truly thankful. The mourners stand protected in a tent. The priest holds down the pages of the Bible against the wind. The cars stand motionless. He pushes a button, a whirring begins and the small pine coffin sinks into a hole. She'll be cold in there. My God, the melted snow will seep through the wood and she'll be cold in there....

'Not even the dogs will answer me now,' Dexter yaps with disgust and kicks the machine back to life. The engine shrieks, lights up, blue lights, orange lights, the headlamp fires a beam at the ocean.

'Hop on,' he says and looks at me strangely. He knows something's up but it makes him uncomfortable and he wants it to go away. That's one of the things I like about him. He's in too much of a hurry to be sad. He likes to take an evening and wring the fun out of it, just like a wash cloth.

We crash back down the road, turn right again, heading further away from the hotel and Franny, further down the deserted coast road. It's getting easier now. We stop at another bar, the Twilight Saloon Inn, and drink more beer. The valium clicks in and I start loosening up. It's two in the morning and that nagging sense of getting back is letting up. I can see the child in her bed, and as long as I can see her in my mind, I know she is safe.

We walked down the road, another hundred yards. The night was spectrally quiet. A BMW raced up from town, its headlights jumping angrily over the road. In the framed windows, blank staring faces. Then they were gone, leaving a cloud of ghostly dust in the air.

No, things really were getting better. A little more time, a little more company. Another beer and then I'd be off. Then I could get a handle on this thing and chart our next move. Maybe the whole thing wasn't such a catastrophe after all. Maybe it was – who knows – a bold stroke. It might be, in J.'s pinched, over-tipping world vision, it might seem like two guys getting drunk and fucking up. But that wasn't it. Not at all. No, this was important ... a voyage, something her tight little face could never understand. Something she'd never do. No, she'd prefer to toddle off to bed with a P. D. James mystery.

And who knows, maybe I never loved her, never wanted her. Maybe she just wore me down and one day I just gave up the ghost and said okay and unlocked the door. Yes, that was it. I left the door open and the wrong dogs came home.

'Is that you talking or the valium?' she might say. Fuck you, Mary-Lou.

The day John Lennon was shot J. walked up the apartment stairway with a bag of groceries. 'Dreadful, isn't it?' she said. I'd just finished washing the dishes and had dropped the silverware indiscriminately into the box, mixing the knives with the forks and spoons. So J. starts talking to me and then notices the silverware; she frowns and, leaving the groceries untouched, starts shuffling through the silverware, putting each piece in it right compartment. She's totally absorbed by it. Don't get me wrong. I wasn't expecting her to burst into tears about John Lennon. She didn't know him or anything. But watching those crisp gestures sort impatiently through the silverware, well, it's true, I did want to give her a cuff across the ear. Fuck you, Mary-Lou.

Funny business that stuff with Lennon though. I was embarrassed to feel as much as I did. I think I cried the next morning over my eggs and I was surprised: it had snuck right up on me.

I remember turning on the radio and moving the dial up and down the channels and it was all I could hear, that great rock'n roll voice, an endearing voice, and you could see him there, feet apart, wailing out 'You Can't Do That' – and doing that funny thing he did with his mouth when he sang as if he's just about to break into a whistle at the end of the phrase – while around him the air exploded with flashbulbs and jelly beans. Not bad for a kid from Liverpool; when you die everyone talks about you and they print your name in lights on the highest building in the world. But you can still hear him, the sardonic reply with the cracked inflection: 'Sure it's great, but it don't beat livin', does it pal?'

Fuck you, Mary-Lou.

Chapter Nine

Dexter had been coming to the island for ten years. When I met him he was living on a forty-foot boat anchored in Montego Bay. Soon after he and the captain had a drunken falling out and the Immigration boys pounced. Dexter was too broke to save himself and they booted him out of the country. A month later he was back. He bought a few drinks, paid off a few debts and the matter was forgotten.

He had many friends, foreigners and 'niggers' alike. His energy and restless appetite for fun drew people to him like a magnet. In the next hour we ran into a handful of his friends. It was like being out on the hustings with a popular candidate and while I didn't meet the girl I'd prayed to meet when we were out in the night-washed field, the new people were at least distracting. There was a tall, bearded Canadian who had recently spent an evening talking to Jack Nicholson; an American lesbian, tanned as a boot, who sold real estate; Bongo, a local ganja dealer and his German girlfriend; two muscular, mustached Quebecois; a pretty, young phoney named Frenchie who billed himself as a

Reuters photographer; a rat-like whore named Mavis; Mr. Peanut, a glib young kid with a peanut franchise and a smile like a sunlamp, and a frazzle-haired woman in her early forties who ran a hotel called Heartbreak. For the most part, they were white, year-round residents, and there was something curiously wrong with all of them – a kind of shared malaise which manifested itself in a very short attention span. They asked you questions – after all it was exciting to have a new face in town, especially now, when the place was shut up like a ghost town – but they didn't listen all the way through to your answers. And no one looked at you very long. They gave the impression of expecting something imminent, that any second it was going to come pedalling along the road or drop out of the sky. But it was disconcerting because it made you feel boring, as if you'd just opened your mouth and already lost your audience. I wondered whether they were all stoned or maybe the sun had tanned something it shouldn't have. But why was nobody in bed? Everyone was up. What could you possibly get at this hour? Why did it seem tonight as if this little Caribbean road throbbed only with misfits, the lonely, the thwarted and the crippled?

'Of course they're not interested in you,' Dexter snorted. 'You don't have anything for them.'

We met some kid in his early twenties, a white kid who'd lost his girlfriend to a local woodcarver and it had made him crazy. He walked up and down the road, hoping for a glimpse of her, running this horror movie through his imagination – 'That's right sonny, her hand around his cock, get it?' – and then denying it, dreaming up outrageous scenarios, anything to dull the excoriating image of them together. He might have been quite exquisite looking, this young prince with the broken heart, but his features were pulled tight in an hysterical mask and you could almost hear the blood pumping in his temples.

'Dexter?' he said, reining himself in to sound off-hand. 'Seen Jane tonight?'

'She's probably at home,' he replied coolly. But the kid wasn't listening.

'I've been looking for her all night. She was going to drop by today. I must have missed her.' Dexter said nothing. The kid turned to me. I was fresh and hadn't heard the story and he wanted to talk about her. He was talking to make himself feel better and because talking about her was a little like being with her and that's as close as he was going to get tonight.

'She's going to get him a work permit,' he explained. 'I mean would you like to work here for the rest of *your* life?'

'It's got its advantages,' I said thoughtlessly and the kid glared hatefully at me. 'I hope you find your friend,' I added softly.

'Right,' he said and walked off.

Dexter eased a toothpick from the corner of his mouth. 'Welcome to Jamaica,' he said.

Chapter Ten

We turned off into Murphy's pool hall, a dilapidated little joint with two wonky tables. They were always crammed, fifteen black guys standing around, smoking cigarettes and shooting lousy pool. The men seemed taller, younger since my last visit. A new generation of guys hanging out in the pool hall. They had their own cues now. One of them was called, seriously, 'the Kid,' and he looked great. Black stove-pipe pants, a hot little red beret; he danced well; he talked well; he held the cue as if he'd been born with it in his mitts. But when it came to shootin' time, he was just about as bad as they come. He was a star of the place though, with those leather moccasins and Bob Marley buttons, and he kept winning.

In the back there was a dining room and it was a good place to eat if you didn't mind waiting an hour for your meal. They served curried goat, fish and conch soup. I like the soup; for two Jamaican dollars they gave you a bowl big enough to bathe a child in. Dexter had a number about the soup. 'Don't eat it,' he'd caution. 'It's full of cats.' I'd never tasted any cats in it. But

I had to eat something. My stomach had a deathly hollow ache.

We pushed our way through the smoky pool hall. The Kid had just demolished another opponent and was doing a little step around the bar. The light was bad. A blinding white bulb hung over each table. The walls were a chipped, boathouse green and they gave everyone a waxen hue, as if they were dead but hadn't stopped moving. There was a couple in the dining room. A stocky man lounged in his chair while a woman sat opposite him in silence.

'You're here!' Dexter exclaimed.

The young woman swung around in her chair and stared right at me. She was rather plain with a long, concave face – a face like a sliver of a one-sixth moon. Pale. Her hair had never been straight enough or curly enough for her satisfaction. It lay uncomfortably in the middle reaching just below her oval chin and gave her a slightly unkempt look. She would have looked better with shorter hair but she didn't like her face enough to risk it. Quite the most attractive thing was her eyes. They were sleepy eyes, as if she had just awoken from a noonday nap. Grey eyes, evocative of eiderdown and Maltese cats.

'Dexter,' exclaimed the man. 'Come over here. Sit down. We were hoping you'd come by. Where are you going?'

'I'm going to the Wharf Club. This guy,' he said

with a jerked thumb in my direction, 'doesn't know *where* he's going.'

The man rose heavily from his chair, sticking out his hand.

'I hope you're not going to ask how the holiday's going.'

'God no,' Dexter replied. 'I'm going to let you buy me a drink. You can talk about anything you want.'

The woman smiled graciously. 'We're just about to eat.'

'Kind of late to eat, isn't it?' Dexter answered, pulling out a chair.

'Jack just woke up,' she said.

'I was having a nap,' he confirmed. He was smashed and he looked sick.

'Have the goat,' Dexter said. 'We'll drink. You eat.'

'Splendid,' enthused the man. He was warming up to the idea of fresh company and more drinks and was absorbed in looking about for the waiter. Probably, as a young man, he'd been quite beautiful, with apple-round cheeks and curly blond hair. Like an angelic Harpo Marx. But something had gone very wrong. He had a boozer's face, jowly and thick and he'd let his body go to pot. He was coarsely overweight. But like his girlfriend his most prominent feature was his eyes. They were big and round and they protruded from his skull like huge marbles. They were dulled by God knows how many things, but they were not stupid.

He caught me staring at him. He wrinkled his brow. 'I'm Jack Miller,' he said, smiling hard and reaching for my hand. I had the feeling that he would have reached right into my pocket and yanked it out. 'Glad to meet you. You know this character I guess?'

'Years and years now,' Dexter said, waving away the issue with his hand. 'Now let's have a drink, shall we? But first. Jack, please. Lend me fifty dollars till tomorrow. I've got money coming in the mail.'

'Let's have a drink first,' Jack hesitated. 'I'll have to have a short one,' he said rubbing his hands together. 'I've got school tomorrow.'

Lily smiled bravely. She could see another 'late dinner' coming but she was being a good sport. Still, she had that look, or I thought she did, as if there was a stop watch ticking in her head, that any day now, it would go click and that'd be the end of Jack. I saw that look in J.'s face, right after the girl in Kansas City.

We weren't alone in the restaurant. Three women sipped beers, waiting to pay for dinner. They were smartly turned out, tanned and articulate. In their middle thirties and well travelled. They reminded me of J.'s friends and I despised them immediately. One of them had a racket-like handle extending from her bag.

'Are you girls tennis players?' Jack asked.

'No,' replied one with red-frame glasses. 'We're swimmers.'

'Then why do you have tennis rackets?'

'That's to hit the fish with.'

Jack issued a windy laugh and addressed the table. 'Sometimes I'm Mary Poppins. Sometimes I'm not....' He faded off. I don't think he could remember the rest of the joke. It was obvious he'd been talking to the women earlier and it was also obvious that while they'd initially found him entertaining, now they were tiring of him. They rose as if on the same breath to leave.

'Bye girls,' he said and looked at me with delight. 'I'm getting blasted.'

'Oi! Black boy! Cisco!' Dexter shouted. Lily stiffened. The bartender materialized in the gloom. We ordered a round of drinks while Lily looked on, slightly sunk in her chair, her face tired and open, a white petal balanced on its edge.

'Four Red Stripe.'

'An Appelton rum for me,' said Dexter.

'White rum,' I said.

'Make that two white rum,' Jack added. 'Lily, have a whack of something.'

'I had a whack last night, Jack. That's why I couldn't get out of bed this morning.'

'She cried,' Jack confided to us.

'I'm not used to drinking rum,' she protested. 'It makes me sentimental.'

'We met a minister,' said Jack.

'He had six kids,' said Lily.

'He also had a toupee sewn on his head. But it was sewn on too low on his forehead.' Jack put his hand over his eyebrows. 'He looked deranged.'

'That wasn't why I was crying.'

'Why were you crying then?'

'I can't remember. This place makes me very sad.'

The drinks arrived and in a flush of enthusiasm Jack addressed me. 'Well Gene-bo, what do you do stateside?' Gene-bo? That was a nightmare even my aunt Gracie hadn't come up with and she had a penchant for obnoxious nicknames.

'I write for a living,' I said, and goddamn if the words didn't back right up in my throat. Liar, liar, pants on fire. Why were those words so impossible to say with a straight face?

'Ever been published?' Lily shot back.

'Sure. Lots of things.' God help me, let's not get into a discussion of that. I didn't want to talk about my grade twelve poetry prize anymore. I could have said, 'Me? Write? You bet ya. I'm so good my ex-wife just canned me after one season.' But we know where the conversation goes after that. 'Right in the shitter,' as Dexter puts it. He's got a flair for words himself.

Jack looked at me shrewdly. The fog lifted briefly from his eyes. My arm throbbed like a pang of conscience.

'This is great,' he said. 'Jamaica is a blessed place. My father came here to die with a woman on each arm.

He lived another twenty-five years.' He tossed off his drink.

'You know, Gene,' he said, 'I write too. Under a pseudonym. I'm a bit of a musician too. Songwriter.'

'He practises law under a pseudonym as well,' Lily interjected.

'I do a little business for my mother.'

'He churns condominiums for her.'

'Never mind,' he said confidently, 'it pays me money every time she changes her mind.'

'I'm a lawyer too,' Lily said.

'And a damn good one,' he added. 'If I got into trouble, I'd hire her. She's tough.'

'Actually it's not that exciting. I do litigation mostly,' she confessed. 'But I love it. I love going to work.'

'I've got a law degree from Harvard,' Dexter said. 'A forgery of course, but you can't tell the difference. It's perfect. I'll show it to you sometime.'

'It's a stuffy firm,' Lily went on, 'but I like it.'

Jack sat up excitedly. 'At the office picnic last year ...' he started in.

'Jack, don't tell that story. It makes me furious.'

'It's funny.'

'Don't bother. It cost me a partnership.' To us, she said, 'It wasn't confirmed yet but they were going to invite me.' She looked at Jack. 'Boy, I thought there was no way back after that one.'

'Stuffy old farts,' he said.

Outside, in the street, a dog coughed. Lily dismissed what she was going to say. 'Jack, I'd like to eat. You know the business with the knives and forks?'

'Come on, Lily. Look on the bright side of things. I've been here almost two hours and I haven't pissed on the dishes yet.' Despite herself she laughed.

'Dexter,' she said, 'where can I get the best lobster in town?'

Deadpan, he raised a short arm and pointed towards the ocean. 'Out there,' he said.

'Really, Jack,' she insisted. 'Why don't you eat something? I'd recommend the soup. Ask them to put it in a glass for you. You won't notice the difference.'

'It'll slow me down. Besides, fish makes me pass wind.'

'Have the goat then.'

'Goat makes me pass wind too.'

Four dew-damp beers arrived with two plastic glasses of white rum.

'I can smell it from here,' Lily grimaced. 'It looks like embalming fluid.'

'I shat my pants for two days the first time I had it. Exploded at both ends. I'll never touch it again,' Dexter said.

'Honestly, Jack,' Dexter continued, 'if you're going to drink that stuff, drink it with water. It'll burn out your stomach. Even the niggers know that.'

'Cheers,' Jack said, swallowed the shot and quickly put down the glass. He sat very, very still. 'Christ!' he whispered.

'Take some water, Jack.'

He took a sip from the jug but it didn't work. With odd formality he excused himself from the table, stepped carefully out the back and retched loudly. Lily didn't move, didn't even look in his direction. 'Your hangover notwithstanding,' I began, 'how are you finding Jamaica?' Awkward question, awkwardly phrased. How long have I been speaking English?

'I've been anxious and guilty since I got off the plane,' she said. 'I keep meaning to enjoy myself. We went to Fort Lauderdale before here. I liked it better. Not so much fuss.'

Cisco came out from the kitchen and looked into the backyard. A slow chuckle. 'Him ago dead.'

'No sir, Cisco. He's like a dog. He does this every night,' Dexter said. He was enjoying the show. He took a deep drag off his cigarette and coughed it up. I couldn't take my eyes off Lily. Lovely shoulders. I wanted her to stand up. I wanted to see the rest of her. I hoped it wasn't too good. Not this again. Damn. Now I'll have to stay. Tired, grey eyes.

'I just hope the kids don't slip in it,' she said cheerfully.

I laughed long and loud. I might as well have worn a

sandwich board with a green light painted on the front.

Jack returned gingerly to the table. 'Sorry everyone,' he announced with an almost English joviality. 'Empty stomach. Too much gas in the beer.' He looked sweaty green.

'Are you going to Savanna-la-Mar tomorrow?' Dexter asked Lily. 'There's a fellow up there I've been waiting three years to see.'

But she wasn't listening. I felt someone staring at me and when I looked up it was her. And then she smiled. But it was more than a smile. It was a beam, an extraordinary beam of good humour and conspiracy. It said, 'I know what you're really like and I think it's great.' She couldn't have surprised me more if she'd thrown a chair at me. I got that queasiness in the pit of my stomach, like the elevator cable just snapped.

Jack had cleaned himself out and now he was ready for another drink.

'Where is that guy?' he groaned. 'I think I've been cut off.'

Dexter cackled. 'They don't cut you off here Jack. They just bury you.'

'No,' he insisted. 'It's deliberate. I think he's fucked off on purpose.'

'Why don't we order some food, Jack?'

He glared at her and stood up.

'I wouldn't do that if I were you,' Dexter warned

'They don't like you serving yourself here.'

Jack craned his neck around. 'Jesus Christ,' he said. He was working himself into a temper.

'Jack,' Lily began, 'I'm sure he's too tired to bother cutting you off.'

He ignored her and she continued with a kind of numb patience. 'He probably sits in a kitchen that's two hundred degrees and he doesn't feel like running out here every five seconds to check on your beer.'

'You were the one who wanted to eat.'

'You're right,' she said conciliatorily. 'What shall we have? Gene, will you join us?'

The question wasn't a difficult one but it caught me unprepared. 'I've already had dinner. But I might have something. I don't know.'

'Doesn't matter,' she said. 'You can have something off my plate, if you change your mind.'

'Good,' said Jack. 'I'm going to have the snapper.'

Dexter: 'They've never heard of snapper here. It's barracuda or goat.'

Jack wasn't listening. 'And I'll have it with dark rum. That's the antidote.'

'Do you know what, Jack?' Lily said. 'I'd like to go to a movie.'

'Ever been to a movie in this country?' Dexter broke in. 'It's berserk. They shout all the way through. They think it's really happening. They showed *Earthquake* and *The Towering Inferno* in Sheffield last year. They called it Shake 'n' Bake.'

Jack frowned. He didn't want anyone else being funny. But Lily was a veteran at this. When she sensed him glowering at her – she didn't need to look – she asked without missing a beat, 'What do you mean an antidote, Jack?'

He began hotly: 'You drink the bloody rum so you won't die. Because the old snappers are full of poison. They get old; they get full of poison. So you drink the rum to neutralize the poison.'

Dexter again mildly: 'I think you mean barracuda.'

'I mean Red Snapper!'

'I think Dex is right,' Lily offered. 'I think I heard it was barracuda.' Thunderous silence.

'Where did you hear it was Red Snapper, Jack?'

It was a brave effort on her part but it's a fine line with a drunk like that. She was covering for him – like some dim-witted kid who'd peed on the carpet – and he knew it.

'Okay,' he said methodically. 'Let's stop making believe. It was a stupid mistake and if I wasn't so pissed....'

'Jack, no one is suggesting....'

'Shut up, Lily.'

'Don't tell me to shut up.'

Dexter groaned and we sat like four strangers in an all-night bus depot.

Chapter Eleven

Cisco's two kids swooped in from the back yard. The taller of the two – he was ten – held a dead sand-crab in his fingers and he was chasing his sister with it. They howled with delight, racing around the tables and back into the night. Lily followed them with her eyes. And stared after them when they were gone. 'They're having such fun,' she said.

'You look sick, Lily,' Jack said, 'Do you want to leave?'

'Last night,' she started, 'that minister asked me if I was a hypochondriac. I said I thought about dying all the time but never about being sick. I suppose that doesn't make me a hypochondriac, does it?'

A car drove by, its right blinker on.

'You know,' Jack began, as if he'd weighed the matter carefully, 'I don't really like this place.' He took a plug from Lily's beer and washed it around his mouth. 'It's like some rotting tennis club. Some piece of shit left over from British colonialism.'

'It is, actually,' Dexter agreed.

'They should give it back to the dogs. Which reminds me. If one of those sons of bitches looks at me the wrong way tonight, I'm going to brain him.'

'They bark at everyone,' I said.

'I don't care.' He was starting to sound like the bicycle nut in the airport. The dogs were conspiring against him. They didn't understand who he was. No ordinary borracho stumbling up the road. To make matters worse, I'd half undressed his wife and the two of us were living in a little cottage in Wales.

When somebody like Jack disintegrates in front of you it's tempting to think you've captured the truth about him, that he's the sum of all the unattractive things you catch him doing: the armour cracks and you get a glimpse of the *real* asshole lurking behind. But it couldn't be that simple. Although there must have been some great magic – or something that passed for magic – between those two, Jack and Lily, what it was I never saw that night. Why was she still here, fidgeting with her hair and loathing him? Why did she stay? Why did J. stay?

I used to tell J. I didn't understand why great women fell in love with awful men. She found that amusing. 'People stay together,' she would say, with a gin and tonic in her hand, 'because they have short memories and shallow, intense feelings.' I don't believe she meant that but, in any case, in the next half hour, Jack went right down the toilet, all hands aboard. He tried to rally, to win back his audience. But he was too smashed. He was catch-up drinking after a second wind but it eluded him. He started in about pissing on the dishes again and that pushed him to greater excess, more strained stories that rambled without a point, jokes that weren't funny, sexual innuendo that left everyone looking away and lighting cigarettes. He just couldn't leave it alone. It was remarkable to watch even if you didn't want to steal his wife. He was compelled to stuff every silence with his personality. He had to be on top, whether he could hold his balance there or not. He ordered more drinks. He wasn't getting plastered anymore. The booze was opening some mineshaft in his personality. It was as if he was determined to betray himself, his intelligence, his wife, everything before he toddled off to bed.

Lily retreated, finally, into a clutch of beers, hastily drunk. Was that what had happened the previous night at the minister's? Dexter didn't care but Jack wasn't going out quietly. He was dominating the table, spoiling Dexter's good time and stepping on his punch lines. Also Jack, old sport, hadn't forked over the fifty bucks yet. As for me I found myself imagining all sorts of things with Lily, most of them in a dark room. Jack was going over the top, I was sure of that. And that would leave her.

I felt like a buzzard perched on a branch in the African veldt. It's true. One approving glance from her and I'd imagined the two of us growing old together.

Dexter was feeding him rope. He leaned back in his chair, his red face slightly mocking, while Jack held the spotlight. 'I shouldn't really be eating this,' he said, taking a forkful of curried goat and stuffing it into his mouth. 'It's going to kill my momentum. I'm going to nod off and somebody's going to snatch my wife. Snatch my wife's snatch.'

Dexter jumped in. 'Well, in a hundred years, Jack, who'll care about a fuck?' He laughed at his own joke and with a little sigh of satisfaction reached across the table to pick a french fry off Jack's plate. Brutishly, Jack clamped a hand over Dexter's wrist and picked up a ketchup bottle. Lily lunged forward with both hands. 'Jack!'

'I don't like people eating my food.' His face was deathly white and calm.

'All right! All right!' Dexter yelped and yanked back his hand. He wanted to play it for a joke but he was shaken and there were four painful, white finger marks on his wrist. Jack must have had the grip of a gorilla. It was an ugly bullying show of strength. He looked like a demented child and I sensed that something terrible was going to happen to him. He was going to push and push and one night, fifteen scotches later, he was going to do something that would ruin his life. There was going to be an 'accident' and he'd burn down his house or stick a knife in someone or smash up his car and kill a kid.

Lily was on her third beer and Jack munched his dinner in silence. Anger gave way to remorse. I could feel him unwinding.

'Dexter,' he said finally, 'I'm sorry. Let me buy you a drink.'

'What are we celebrating?'

'Oh God. I'm getting tired. That goddamn goat is making me tired. I'm going to have to get the hell out of here.'

'Have you got the keys or do I?' Lily asked. I took up my drink and took a sip to disguise my excitement. Jack surveyed her fuzzily. Dexter, I noticed, paid unabashed attention. I liked him a great deal at that moment. He looked amused and pissed off and curious and funny, all at once. I tried to look noncommittal, innocent even, as if these goings-on were a mystery to me. But it was a mask that wouldn't stay put; it kept slipping off and I wondered if Jack saw my hooked beak and blood-matted feathers.

'I've got the keys but you're coming too,' he said.

'No, I'm not,' she said flatly. 'Are you going to smash me with a ketchup bottle?'

Jack looked visibly hurt. A low blow. How could she bring up the past and hurl it in his face like that?

'Come on, Dex. Let me buy you a drink.'

'I've already got a bloody drink.'

'Dexter,' he said, as one might to a truculent child

who didn't want to come out of the cupboard. 'I'm going to buy you a drink.'

'He doesn't want a drink, Jack! And why are you being such an asshole?'

'Then you buy him a drink,' he sighed towards Lily. 'For God's sake, somebody buy somebody a drink.' He reached into his pocket and pulled out a stack of red folded bills and counted off three. He was very careful with his money, careful not to bend it or tear it. Looking at those hands I had the notion that a lot of money had gone through them.

'Here's sixty bucks, Dexter. Pay it when you can. All right? Am I forgiven?'

Dexter wasted no time stuffing the bills into his shorts.

'Okay,' Jack said, 'I'm ready. I can't keep my eyes open.'

'Sure you can,' she said.

'No,' he insisted, 'I'm so drunk I can't say barbecue.'

He was sitting up straight now, trying a new routine. The good sport routine. It said:

'Look everybody, I can take a joke. I'm a regular guy and this is fun.' But he hated every moment of it and he couldn't wait to get her alone and get even.

'Ask me anything,' he said with a broad smile and a quizzical, little-boy expression. 'I'm having a ball.' I wondered if he might be a little crazy.

133

'Go on,' he repeated. 'Ask me something.'

'Say barbecue.'

'Barbecue. But you're not taking me seriously, Lily, and if I remember this in the morning, I'm leaving.' He guffawed at his own joke.

'Have a drink,' she said. 'You wanted one. So drink, because now I'm in the mood.'

'You're slammed, baby.'

And then the lights went out. Literally. In the bulbs over our heads, in the neighbouring shacks, in the bright chain of coloured lights up and down the road, the light vanished as if a gush of ocean wind had extinguished the flame from the entire island. We were left in candlelight.

'Let's go outside for awhile, Lil,' Jack whispered.

'I like it here,' she replied. 'I'd like to go somewhere where the bartender can tie a knot in the stem of a maraschino cherry with his tongue.' The three top buttons of her shirt were undone and it opened when she leaned forward and in the candlelight I could see where her tan stopped.

'For Christ's sake,' Jack burst out angrily. 'Are you staying or going?'

'I don't know. Am I staying?'

A nightmare of physical jealousy sat blood-red in front of him. He stood up hastily, as if pushing away the thought. Lily looked at him with a smile of embarrassment and bewilderment. 'Are you off?'

'Yes. And you?'

I waited. Dexter waited. He waited. And when she answered it sounded like she had just taken her voice out of the icebox.

'You have the key.'

Chapter Twelve

Lily, Dexter and I headed down the road. On a clear night like this, the people across Twelve Mile Bay can hear you talking in your sleep but Dexter shouted over his shoulder anyway: 'God,' he roared, 'I sure hate to be broke in niggertown. You can do anything in this town except owe people money.'

The green lights of a deserted American hotel glowed across the sound. The power had come back on. As we passed the dogs were silent, watching with diamond-bright eyes. A young woman came walking briskly towards us. She had her head down and was moving at a very good clip. She almost ran into us before she stopped with a little shriek of surprise. In the streetlight I saw that her face was red from too much sun.

'You startled me,' she said, spooked. There wasn't anyone following her but she had that special step of manic purpose. No time to stop and talk. Keep on moving, one foot in front of the other. Anxiety spreading like a prairie fire. Probably she had no idea what it was about – a careless word earlier that day, a misplaced plane ticket, the man in the bar who never came back; it was just something and it was really bugging her. I bet she marched all the way to town like that and then turned and marched all the way back. A couple of nights like this and she'd think she'd really lost her marbles. Her panic was contagious and I picked it up like a tuning fork. Just the sight of her set off a whole barrage of kicks and thumps under the blanket of valium, beer and overproof. Maybe I should have said something to her but she was too jumpy and too unattractive. There was no time for detours. A kindred spirit maybe, but not tonight. Doppelgänger-schmoppelgänger.

'How are you tonight?' Lily asked kindly.

'Fine thanks,' came the reply. 'Everything is just fine, thanks. Thank you and goodnight.' Her red face revolved, was replaced by a knotted bun of hair and she hurried back up the road.

A red taxi pulled to a stone-churning halt. 'You want a taxi, mister?' lamented a woman's voice, a Jamaican voice, as red as the car. It surprised me, and I stepped out of the shadows towards the car door and looked inside. A red cigarette ember burned in the back seat.

'Why no thank you,' I said. 'But thanks for stopping.'

'You want to stay with me tonight?'

'No thank you, ma'am.'

'Come to my house, tall man.'

'No, I can't. Really. I'm married.'

'That your wife?' she asked quietly, glancing at Lily.

'No. My wife is coming tomorrow.'

'Then why can't I stay with you tonight?'

'Because I'm with a friend tonight,' I said. 'Besides, I'm deathly hungover.'

'Then go to the hospital,' she teased. 'If you're sick, go to the hospital.'

After a pause I said, 'Besides, I'm the worst fuck on the island and everyone knows it.'

'It's true,' Dexter snorted from the side of the road. He blew his nose out of the side of his hand.

The woman giggled softly. 'Bring it over here,' she said, reaching her hand out the window. 'Bring it here. Let me just see it.' The arm waved languorously from the car and blew back down the road.

Soon we stopped again. Bertie's Lobster Bar, a brightly lit roadside joint, three or four black guys shouting at each other, nobody behind the bar, a sign 'No gossipers or idlers' tacked up in the doorway. Everything at a complete standstill. We waited at the bar as an old man came in behind us. 'Nobody?' he asked the empty counter with a sweet voice. He tapped a bony hand on the counter top. The old flesh smacked lightly, bird bones through thin skin. 'Nobody,' he said again.

And then a girl came out, dumpy-waisted and big-bummed. She stood in front of us and said nothing. The old gent ordered a white rum. She took a frosted Gilbey's gin bottle from the cooler and set it in front of him. There was dew running down the side and it made my mouth water. She poured a shot of overproof – there was the smell again – into a black-tinted shot glass, let it run over the brim and dumped it into a glass. He added a little water. I needed a pick-me-up. The hangover was closing in like a shark over my shoulder. I ordered a white rum and a beer chaser. The old man grinned approvingly. He took four rums a day himself and he was 92. I wished I had a grandfather like him, those lovely pink hands brushing crumbs from his Sunday vest.

When the beer arrived I grabbed the bottle by the ass end, and poured down a couple of big gulps. Lily looked slightly preoccupied and I thought she was thinking about Jack. Good-naturedly, she asked, 'You didn't mention your wife was coming tomorrow.'

You could tell she found the notion slightly offensive, not my being married, but the fact that I hadn't mentioned it. In her polite, eastern seaboard way, she was turning over the new information in her mind and you could almost hear the flutter as her new perceptions were shuffled into a fresh deck. And I didn't like what I thought was emerging, an image of myself as a tipsy salesman knocking off a last piece in Pokipsieville before the short leg home.

'My wife divorced me a hundred years ago,' I said. 'She doesn't even know where I am.'

'Oh,' she said softening.

Dexter, never one to miss an opportunity, pressed the advantage.

'He's got a daughter too. She's already here,' he responded gleefully, as if to say forget him, he's got too much baggage. It worked quite the reverse. Lily found that enchanting, a dad and his daughter on vacation.

'You hardly ever see it,' she said. 'Maybe we could all go swimming together?'

What a capital idea!

'Jack and I were supposed to take the bus to Savanna-la-Mar tomorrow. I guess that's off now,' she said almost privately.

'Savanna-la-Mar,' Dexter hooted. 'I'll tell you a story about Savanna-la-Mar. I went to the Wharf Club one night when I first got to Jamaica and God did I get drunk. At four o'clock in the morning one of the bartenders stabbed the other in the neck with an ice pick. Shoved it right in to the handle. And the girl went screaming-nuts into the street with this thing hanging from her neck like some kind of a bloody growth. It was the most horrible thing I've ever seen in my life.'

I understood the point of the story because I knew Dexter. The point was: 'Look at me. I have a terribly adventurous life and these things happen to me all the time.' But Lily didn't read it that way. She read it like: 'What a disgusting, pointless story.' I think she knew Dexter took himself as something of a legend and it made her slightly impatient. She found it childish.

After a moment's silence she said, 'What's that got to do with Sav?'

'Oh,' Dexter replied, having already lost interest in the story, 'that's where they took her to the hospital. I don't know what happened to her. I'm going to switch to dark rum. Anyone going to join me?'

As we were about to leave, a mud-coloured man with green eyes eased into the bar. He looked cool and confident.

'Whoops,' Dexter said, spinning back to the counter. 'This is trouble.' He threw a long, calculating glance towards the kitchen, then decided against it. There wasn't anywhere to hide. 'You remember that whore who tore my shirt today?' he whispered. 'That's her husband.'

'Dexter.' The man frowned.

'Michael,' Dexter said.

'Give me the keys to the motorcycle.'

'What motorcycle?'

'Chaw. Don't bullshit me, Dexter. I followed you up from Murphy's. You left it there.'

'I'm not going to give you the keys to anything,' Dexter said, affecting weariness.

A patient hand like a horned glove settled on the bar beside him. 'Give me the key. Don't make me vexed with you.'

Dexter cranked up his nasal voice, blew himself up like a lizard and hollered: 'You're not getting any keys.'

He was perfectly safe yelling and he knew it.

Michael was unruffled. He addressed himself to me. 'You sir. Just stand aside. This has nothing to do with you.' Lily observed quietly.

'You stick me up?' Dexter blustered. 'The police come and lick you down.'

'Me no'teif,' the man said quietly.

'I know the Minister of Tourism. I drank *rum* with him in Bob Marley's house. He'll put your Rasta ass in jail. You'll be making licence plates in Spanish Town.'

The amused and curious Jamaicans in the bar looked on, but then Dexter stepped over the line. 'I'm going to knock your block off,' he said. Michael considered him, his physique, for a moment, and then did something I'd never seen before. He stood straight up, raised his arms to shoulder height and flexed his muscles. It was like watching a kid caught up in a fantasy in the bathroom mirror. Except there was no daydreaming about it. He flexed those muscles and there wasn't enough skin to go around them.

'See here, Mr. Police-spokesman,' he said sternly. 'Try to lick me down and I brutalize your structure.'

CHAPTER TWELVE

Dexter checked himself, closing his mouth.

'All right, all right,' he agreed wearily. 'Don't vex up. God, you people take everything so seriously. How about money?'

The black man scrutinized him.

'You got to pay rent. You can't just quit the house.'

'Forty dollars, sir.'

'No. The keys,' he insisted and stuck out his palm.

'Sixty dollars then. The rest soon,' Dexter promised.

Michael crooked his fingers and Dexter put the three fresh bills he'd just borrowed from Jack into his hand.

After a moment's hush, Dexter groaned. 'I need money,' he said to the hushed room. 'Don't you all need money?' There was no answer. 'Who needs *money*?' he implored. 'I want everyone in this room who needs money to raise his hand.' Michael smiled. Beside him a man went back to his newspaper. Another lit a cigarette. The spell was over.

'That's the thing about this place,' Dexter said when we were on the road again. 'You can't ever relax. Just when you start walking around town like you're the mayor, that's the night you open your bedroom door and wish you'd never been born.' Lily trailed behind us.

To our right was Tiger Bates' empty field. During the season, when the townsfolk were flush with money – and sin – he threw revival meetings there. Under a crescent-shaped tent two hundred souls lifted up their voices to the stars, raised their matchstick arms and polished the moon with pink-palmed hands. But that was months away. Now the field was empty, the tent gone, the wooden chairs gone, the preacher in his powder-blue suit gone. Nothing stirred in that field except the tall grass.

But there was something curious – a rumour of activity in the tree-line. I wondered if they were the spirits of the departed sinners. Music and voices, laughter, candlelight and gas light spilled towards us. A knot of men appeared at the top of the road, where it curved into the jungle. They walked unsteadily down a gravel path. On the seawall, a woman and her sweetly dressed daughter waited. The child's hair was immaculately and precisely parted. She yawned, leaning against her mother's shoulder, careful not to scuff her school shoes against the seawall.

Dexter jumped like a kid who's just remembered it's Saturday.

'The wake,' he said to Lily. 'We *have* to go.' Dexter wasn't speaking to me, or even in my direction. He was talking to Lily and I became uncomfortably aware that he was trying to get rid of me. My old pal Dexter Alexander was trying to give me the slip. I was going to be abandoned here at the fork in the road, or maybe later he was going to lose me in the crowd at the wake. We'd been killing time with each other and now there was a girl and it was time to part.

I took a long look at Dexter. I'd forgotten how shrill and desperate he was. Or so I fancied that night. Maybe it was as simple as both of us going after the same girl. I felt like I was holding onto Lily's shirt sleeves with invisible fingers and imploring her to stay.

Lily hesitated.

'Come on,' he cajoled her. 'Have a short one and a quick look at the old gal. They've got an open coffin, don't you know?'

He stood back on the balls of his feet. He was pushing too hard and I don't think she liked him anymore. As a matter of fact I suspected that she'd never really liked him, certainly not since she'd heard him holler out 'black boy' at Cisco's. She had a dainty sense of civil liberties and no matter how much wit you wrapped around the word 'nigger' she just didn't find it funny.

Dexter was, in her eyes, just a pain-in-the-ass who never listened to anyone – just the sort Jack was always 'discovering' and dragging home with him after the bar closed.

'I want to go to the Wharf Club,' she said. 'Wasn't that the plan?'

'I've got to meet someone up there,' Dexter said. 'He owes me money.'

'What about you?' he said to me.

'I want to Wharf it,' I said. Dexter was locked in now. 'I'll be ten goddamn minutes,' he growled over his shoulder as he set off across the field towards the men. 'Wait for me.'

Lily and I sat on the seawall, a short distance from the woman. She was preoccupied again and the silence was making me more and more self-conscious. Now that I had this woman alone, I couldn't think of anything to say to her. Like an old whore going through her wardrobe, I simply couldn't find a dress I hadn't fucked someone in. Who am I supposed to be in this conversation? When she says Gene, who's she talking to? I'd sure hate to come flying out of the closet in the wrong costume.

'Do you think Jack found his way home?' I asked.

'Like a salmon,' she said.

Another silence.

'I *do* like your friend Dexter,' she said, reading my thoughts. 'He's very funny. I just can't imagine fucking him though,' she added matter-of-factly. I checked to see if a mean spirit lurked behind the remark but it didn't.

'He makes me kind of sad, your friend Dexter.'

As soon as I said it I was sorry. 'He makes me kind of sad too.' I winced as the words came out of my mouth. Dexter? Make me sad? Not even close. I make me sad, life makes me sad, but not Dexter. He never makes me sad. 'But I don't know him very well,' I added.

That was even better. Not only stupid but a coward as well.

'Do you plan to have more children?' Lily asked.

'Sure.'

'Let's face it,' she said very harshly after a moment. 'Women do ninety-nine percent of the work anyway.'

I didn't think she was talking to me so I wasn't offended.

'Not in my case,' I said mildly. She made a face.

'Maybe,' she said.

I wanted to argue the issue but after the last twenty-four hours, I wasn't comfortable speaking out on fathers' rights.

'How long have you and Jack? ...'

She cut me off pleasantly. 'I don't want to talk about Jack anymore.'

'Would you like to head off to the Wharf Club?'

'This is silly,' she said. 'I should go home.'

It was all disintegrating around me now. Lily was slipping, the island was slipping. I looked up and down the road. It wasn't the same road I remembered. Something magic used to happen on this road and now, when I needed it, there seemed, after all, very little to it. It had become, from where I sat beneath the increasingly margarine-coloured moon, a little trail twisting through a tourist town. What superstition I had brought to this road, that it ran like an artery through the centre of my life, what self-deluding nonsense. I shouldn't have come back here. I should stop coming back to these old places and old people. No more shrieking phones in the night, my voice full of old times rolling through the line: 'That was great! Let's do it again.' Maybe I should leave the dead alone, the coffins closed. Maybe I should unclench my fingers for a second and let the world escape.

But like my daughter, I sometimes feel the world just lets you get warmed up and then sends you to bed. 'Do it again,' she cries, ecstatically, 'do it again.' A bounce on your lap, a cop with a whistle, a clown with balloons on his finger. It doesn't matter to Franny. She just wants *more*. And so do I. I wish I'd been in the Beatles. I wish I'd been in *Last Tango in Paris*. I wish I'd left the party, just once, before the host went to bed. Indeed, sitting here, I have the sensation of having just arisen from the table where once again I have eaten too much, my only moments in absentia, so to speak, being those spent around back with my finger down my throat, making room for the next course. God forbid there should be a few untouched canapés or a nugget of pâté de foie gras. But I have done it again, haven't I? The band has gone home, and there's a cigarette butt floating in the champagne bucket and I'm still here, propped up like the palace scarecrow.

I have a favourite terrible memory and it goes like

this: J. races down the stairs after me, catches up with me in the doorway, grabs my arm, her hand shaking and her mouth dry, and she says: 'Please don't go over there tonight. Just not tonight. I can't stand the thought of you in her bed.' Her voice breaks with fear like an adolescent's. I yank my arm free and run out the door and down the glistening street and Christ, the fear in her voice, I can still hear it sometimes at three o'clock in the morning, this shakey voice behind me as I run up the street and drop the coffin lid across both our hearts.

I wish to God I'd gone back to Chinatown that night. Tiptoed up the stairs, back into her bedroom, put my hand on her shoulder and told her I was back. I could have turned my whole life around.

Anyway fuck it. I didn't. And what does it matter anyway, who did what to whom, who came through and who didn't? Nobody could care less anymore and none of these thoughts is worth having. I've pushed myself to extraordinary lengths to find myself in the company of some pretty road-weary pensées. And where am I going to get another beer? And why doesn't this woman speak, say something, keep me better company? Why do I have to make the chat? Why is it always the guy?

I feel myself slipping into a quiet back-burner rage. There's nothing new here, is there? Just the same old stuff, get me a drink or get me a girl. Groin or gullet, gullet or groin. The same threadbare furniture rear-ranged by a senile aunt. I'm starting to bore even myself.

I look at Lily. Yep, I want her too. Just like I wanted the Israeli on the bus. And the stewardess on the plane.

God, those girls. The fucks, the hugs, the grabs, the scratches, the hot breath, the soaked jeans, the soaked shirt tails, the frantic delicious sweat of a girl on a warm July night. I can't think of a time, ever, when they didn't jar me off balance, leave me damp-palmed with self-consciousness and my heart throbbing visibly in the side of my neck. Back there in grade two, I'm standing out behind the school house, motionless, and I'm watching the girls as they flutter across the play-ground, these little white dresses with butterscotch faces. Those girls. It was like that even from the begin-ning. Hypnotic. Obsessive.

Which brings us to the girl I dumped J. for. She was a pretty girl with a long ballerina neck, gliding through the darkness with a tray of margaritas. Night after night, while the bar phone rang and the bartender said I wasn't there, I watched my swan-necked friend as she went about her awful business. 'I hate my job,' she'd say. 'I wish I was in the movies, like your wife.'

After hours, I'd sit at table 24 when she counted her tips. 'I'm going to be an actress.' 'I'm going to be a writer.' 'I want to dance with the Bolshoi.' Wishes like the smoke from her cigarette, breaking on the ceiling and fanning into the back alley.

'I'm going to be an astronaut.'

'Of course you are baby, but hey, this is hot-dog mustard. I said *Dijon!*'

Once I made a tipsy ascent up her fire escape at three o'clock in the morning. I fancied it was the most courageous thing I'd ever done and a couple of hours later the whole banal scenario played itself out. But to be fair, who's to say that my actress, dancer, waitress, astronaut girlfriend didn't get the poopy end of the stick? Who's to say that when she saw me bent over the refrigerator, my bum poking out from under the towel, stuffing the last crumbs of banana cake into my mouth, she didn't feel a tad gypped? Maybe that's not what she had in mind when she was fourteen and ran out of the house on a Saturday night, tingling with excitement.

One boozy night, in a jealous rage, I ripped out a handful of her hair and clobbered her over the head with the telephone. Sometime later she pushed me down a flight of stairs and broke my arm. That was the slaughterhouse I ran back to that night in Chinatown.

I remember once there was a little girl in my grade nine class. She was a mousey little thing with no chin and a squeaky voice and she'd written a poem about love. She was very shy and it was agonizing for her to read out loud. Anyway she made it all the way through the poem – you could hear her taking these little mousey breaths between verses – all the way to the last line which went, 'And say it was love I died for.'

Twenty years later, when I think of my martini-toting friend and her blood-splattered telephone, I remember my little poet and I fantasize running into her on the street. I'd say to her: 'Boy, that sure was one *hell* of a last line!' Now I know it's normal for young girls to imagine themselves dying of a broken heart – young boys too – and I'm not kidding myself that she'd remember the poem or me but I fancy she'll remember the occasion, that breathless public reading, because she was on her way up that afternoon. Anyway, I'd love to hear now what she has to say about this business of croaking for love.

But she's gone. J.'s gone, the cocktail waitress is gone. Just old dusty pants here, looking for a pal. But thinking back on it, since that night in Chinatown, I've been giving J. a twist in my imagination, turning her into something she'd hate. I don't want to tell stories out of school but old J., she stepped out a bit in her time too. When she hits her stride she can push the needle right off the tart meter. I remember her visiting me in the hospital. We were in our twenties then, just babies really. It turned out I'd picked up a nasty virus in Mexico, had a whopping fever and felt like I was going to die. J. popped around to the hospital, breezed past my girlfriend who was fluttering indecisively in the hallway and gave me a blow job that just about put me in my grave. It was her way of saying goodbye I guess – Saint J. administering the last rites. And when it was over she ushered in my girlfriend with such solemnity I laughed out loud.

Indeed J. *was* a hard woman to say no to. Once she decided she wanted you, it was easier to pry a crustacean off a rock than get her to change her mind. Reciprocity had nothing to do with it. She'd just show up at your door and refuse to leave. She'd kind of sneak up on you in the wee hours of the morning, pretend to fall asleep on your bed or need a moment's rest before getting out of the car. So you'd sit there and suddenly, softly, those long fingers of hers found themselves settled in your lap like the family cat. You were already halfway there. Then it was your turn to pretend nothing was happening. Wind down the window, gaze thoughtfully at the ceiling and then, well, that was that. Before too long she was in your bed and then in your heart.

I sit by the side of the road and feel myself descending into tearful morbidity. It comes face-up to meet me, slowly, rising like bubbles through India ink. Franny, the child with the rosebud mouth, sleeps forever.

In the jungle a dog barks like a saxophone riff. What if it rains tomorrow? What will Franny and I do? Sit in a damp room and watch for the rainbow across the

bay? Scratch sand-fly bites and talk about J.? There are
no pens or paints or coloured markers in this hotel, no
drawing paper, no television, no kiddies' books. What
five-year-old wants to sit in a stifling room and listen to
a thirty-four-year-old man agonizing about his life?
God, what shall we do if it rains tomorrow?

Chapter Thirteen

'Come on,' I said to Lily. 'Dexter's been fifteen minutes.' But she deferred a second time. It was beginning to feel like a date that's not working out, as if I was going to have to persuade her every ten yards to stay with me. The prospect exhausted me and I realized I couldn't keep auditioning all night long. It would wear me to a frazzle and I'd probably never get her anyway.

'Lily.' I stood up with an authentic sigh of weariness and disappointment and fading booze. 'I'm going to the Wharf Club now.' It could have been a very awkward moment when you both drop your glance, but this time instead of looking away I looked right at her, right at her hair line and then right into her eyes. I didn't smile but I didn't *not* smile either. Well, I thought, you'll have to do something, make some tiny, insignificant gesture or I'm just going to let it go. But the funny thing was I was thinking it in the nicest way; just okay if you're not sure you want me maybe you're right and maybe you should make the decision for both of us. And Lily stared right back at me and then jumped down off the wall and followed me down the road.

As we passed under a spotlight, she stopped me.

'Your arm's bleeding,' she said. 'What have you done to yourself? Let me see.' I peeled back the bandage.

'My God!' she gasped. 'How did you do that?'

'I stuck it through a window.' After a pause I added unwisely, 'Actually I did it on purpose.'

'What?' There was a hard, self-protective edge to her voice. Lily wasn't the kind of girl who was intrigued by or even passingly interested in psychotic shenanigans. I back-pedalled.

'One of those glass doors. I didn't see it until too late.'

'Does it hurt?'

'No, the doctor gave me something for that.'

'Oh. Is that why you're slurring?'

'Am I slurring?'

'Sometimes.'

'Oh.'

Slurring?

'I must have pulled at the stitches.'

'Here.' She handed me a wad of folded serviettes from her back pocket. 'They're clean. I nicked them from the Sheraton. I was saving them for our hotel. They never have any toilet paper.' I tucked a piece of the serviette in under the dressing and pulled back the bandage. Abruptly Lily yawned. 'I need a second wind.'

'Aren't you hot under that sweater?' I asked.

'I'm just fine thanks.'

By the side of the road, under a cone-shaped spotlight, we came across a green shack the size of a double outhouse. Inside stood a high dark wood counter, a shelf of biscuits, beer bottles and soda pop.

In the shade a girl drowsed in a hammock, one leg on the floor.

'Don't wake her up,' Lily said.

'I have to.'

'Hello,' I whispered. 'Hello.' The girl opened her eyes, reached over and fiddled with the knob on an oversized chrome gleaming tape deck. I wondered if the Israeli girl had sold it to her. The radio beamed in crackling calypso on two different channels. I shook my head.

'It's okay. We're not staying. I just need a beer.'

The girl lay back in the hammock and clicked off the radio. She closed her eyes, as if in relief, and lay for a moment to collect her thoughts, running a dry brown hand over a dry mouth and then heffed herself onto her feet and stepped around back of the counter. You could hear the ice bucket open and she settled a couple of cold beers on the counter.

'I'm fuckin' sick and tired of Jamaican music,' she said, smiling sleepily.

'We could have waited till the Wharf Club,' Lily remonstrated.

'I couldn't.' I picked up the bottle. 'You're going to have to excuse me.'

I turned my back on them and drank three-quarters of the bottle in one gulp. The bubbles burnt the back of my throat and my eyes watered.

'Now I ask you,' I said jubilantly, 'do I have a drinking problem or what!'

'It's okay,' answered the woman.

Lily scrutinized me. A vague squint of disapproval.

'You know,' she said, 'you don't look so hot. You really look like shit in here.'

I didn't have an answer for that one but I did have a cold beer and I felt better already. Just the knowledge that there was more to drink nearby cheered me up. The woman slippered her way back to the hammock and we set off again.

'I'm half drunk,' Lily said sourly. 'There's nothing worse.'

'Any chance we'll run into Jack tonight?' I asked.

'Why?' she replied stonily. There was that tone again, hard and it hurt me. And that in turn irritated me. In the first blossom of confidence which comes from having downed almost an entire beer, I felt somewhat self-righteously that I deserved better. And yet there was something agreeable about the annoyance, something quite liberating. It made me want her less and the less I wanted her the less intimidated I was about her leaving.

'You know Lily,' I began. 'I find that tone of yours rather trying. It makes me feel like dumping you at the side of the road and saying goodnight.'

'Oh, don't do that,' she bounced back. 'Still, it's too bad that Jack's already met you. It'd be fun to tell him about you.'

The remark disarmed me, perhaps a little too easily, like the pretty girl who blows you a kiss and your armour clanks to the floor.

To the right of us, half a mile into the hills you could see the villas. They twinkled and glittered, their compounds guarded by dogs and spotlights; rows of waist-high cement boxes where restless Dobermans waited. Nothing reached the villas except the music from the shoreline – and eventually the jungle.

We crossed a scrubby patch of land, stepping onto a flat rock the size of a table. The wind picked up dramatically. It blew in exhilarating gusts; rushing suddenly over the seawall, it took your breath away. Pungent washes of salt air and it made you feel like a child when you stuck your head from the car window.

A white man, drunk and shirtless, lurched up behind the seawall. He'd just woken up and stood blinking stupidly, wavering on the balls of his feet, trying to focus. We both jumped. His features were distorted and veiny, that peculiar white rum distortion as if someone had turned up the unhappiness in him. He opened his mouth. Gibberish poured from it like vomit and he opened his eyes wider to help us understand.

When we didn't answer he shrugged a long, exaggerated gesture and moved shakily forward, left, right, left, right.

'Tell me, Lily,' I said, as if to an old chum. (I was feeling great!) 'Do you think about dying all the time?'

'No.' She laughed. 'I just said that because I knew you were listening.'

She halted her step for a moment and said: 'Do you know what the low point of this trip was? When Jack lost his passport and all our money the first night in town. A fisherman found him in tears up in Redground and had to bring him home. And God, did he stink! That's one of my virtues,' she conceded, assuming I was a step ahead of her, 'I like mysterious people but I have no compulsion to be mysterious myself.'

'For example?'

'For example I'm not going to fuck you tonight. There's no mystery there.'

'Not anymore.'

'I didn't take three weeks off work and jeopardize a partnership just to fuck the balls off a stranger. At least I hope I didn't.'

As we were about to cross the road, I rested my hand on the back of her neck. A thin veneer of sweat. You could almost taste the salt. In front of us, a man sat on the seawall, a coked-out Rastafarian with a snake-headed walking stick between his legs. He tapped it on the pavement to catch our attention. I imagine he'd been there for hours, putting the touch on everyone who went by.

Lily, to my surprise, fluttered from beneath my fingers like a bird.

'He works at the hotel,' she whispered, alarmed.

'Lily,' rumbled the snake-man in an affable bass tone.

'Ritchie,' she piped back, in what I guessed was her mother's voice, an octave higher and real phoney baloney.

Ritchie looked at me, then at Lily and laughed. The wise old coot was pretending to have seen it all. And he had. And for ten Jamaican dollars he'd keep his mouth shut. Lily practically skipped over to him. I couldn't be bothered. I'd seen him before. He was a lazy, parasitic turd. But I wondered why Lily had darted away like that: was she afraid that Ritchie was going to snitch on her? I didn't hear what they said to each other, but in a minute she caught up with me.

Ritchie was still watching us, tapping his ninety-nine-cent cane on the sidewalk like the Lion of Judah himself.

'Did you give him any money?' I snorted.

'That man makes me very uncomfortable. Those eyes....'

'Those are coke-eyes, my dear.'

'I just didn't want you feeling me up in front of him.'

So she was sneaking around and it made her feel like a creep. Now I've done a little sneaking around. Once, when Franny was little more than a plump blonde squiggle in a red sweater, she appeared in a movie, a clumsy, lifeless little piece directed by one of J.'s friends. I took the cocktail waitress to the screening, to impress her, I think, but when Franny's name rolled up on the opening credits I heard J.'s laugh and a clap at the back of the house. A solitary clap at the back of the crowded theatre. She wasn't supposed to be there and I stole out before the end of the film, out the back exit, cocktail waitress in tow, and I ran into J. and her impeccably polite, Scottish father in the back parking lot. After that day it was never much fun to sneak around again.

'Isn't there anyone you're afraid to run into?' Lily said defensively.

'My old headmaster,' I said.

'Jack went to one of those dreadful schools too,' she answered. 'Believe me I'm used to overweight men and their lush mothers.'

'Am I overweight?' I replied hastily, clutching myself.

'You don't look like Artaud.'

'No, really, do you think I should lose some weight?'

'You're fine. I'm here, aren't I?'

'Besides I just woke up and I'm always puffy when I wake up.'

'You know what, Gene,' she said, 'I like it when you talk. It makes me want to laugh out loud.' She beamed at me with such affection I could hardly speak and for a second I thought I was in love with her. Wrists brushing wrists on the way to the Wharf Club. But there was that frown again. Something was coming. I felt her body hesitate.

'I can't sleep with you,' she said. 'I think we're rounding fast on the subject.' She went on after a hesitation. 'I could kiss you though. I'd like to do that. I wanted to do it in the restaurant.'

I stiffened a little, but involuntarily. She was a good kisser.

'Oh.' She dropped back. 'You don't like that. That wasn't a good idea?'

'No, it was,' I said. 'I've just been drinking all night. I probably stink of overproof.'

'No, I didn't notice. You taste quite lovely to me. I hope that's not because I smell of it.'

'No, no. Not at all.'

'Let me do it again.'

I couldn't relax. My shoulders were up. I was thinking I wish I had a bathroom – a nice, white porcelain bathroom with a washcloth and soap and thick towels and I could make myself perfect for her. I wanted to put my hand at the very small of her back. And rather clumsily I did. She watched me evenly, and the evenness seemed so devastatingly sexy I wanted to swoon.

'It's very hot back there.' She kissed me again quickly. 'I really can't do this. But I like you so much. Let's go and have that drink.'

I didn't move.

'Look,' she began slowly, 'I can't do anything. I have to go back tonight. Do you understand what I mean? I can't crawl back into his bed smelling like a greenhouse.'

I didn't answer but I did feel a slight irritating twinge of jealousy. Ridiculous, but I didn't care. I couldn't get it out of my head, this idea that it was my last chance at something. The last of the first, sweet, early moments with a woman.

She waited for an answer and when there wasn't one she went on.

'Look, I could do something for you, if you know what I mean. But there'd be nothing in it for me and I don't think you're that kind of man.'

'Yes I am.'

'I'd just be doing it for your sake.'

I cleared my throat. 'I can live with it if you can.'

'Come and have a drink with me. Please.'

And we moved on. The road dipped down, passing close to a sandy beach. A brightly lit English mansion faced the sea. Its wood was grey, salt-corroded, and the windows were barred and black as coal. On the pavement in front of us a crab as round as a pie crossed over, bright orange under the light. And then another. We had come across some kind of crab crossing. Some had been flattened by cars and their shadows lay seared on the pavement, just the outline, the bodies carried off by lines of ants.

Past the road leading up to Redground. Two whores sat against the wall of the Presbyterian church and fastened their eyes on Lily as we walked by. They said nothing but watched her, her clothes, her hair, like passing a Geiger counter up and down her body. Their attention was so strong you could feel it physically.

'I've *got* to find a bathroom,' Lily said. 'I'm frantic.'

Down the road was a hideous new structure which throbbed with disco music. Somebody had bought a patch of land, slaughtered all the vegetation and plopped down a circular bamboo hut. It was garishly lit, with flood lights and sat perched on the water's edge like an attendant's booth in a parking lot.

Dark purple neon burned inside.

A girl danced alone on a tiny dance floor. She was wearing jeans and a sleeveless grey T-shirt with U.S.A. stamped in big curly letters across the front.

We went in.

Inside the circular room a man with a head set, the disc jockey, stood facing the sea through barbed wire. He caught sight of us. I shouted hello at him. Lily approached the bar and took out her wallet. Abruptly she changed her mind and leaving the wallet on the bar disappeared into the back. The d.j., a grey-haired guy in his mid-forties, wandered over and addressed me in Canadian English. His name was Bill. He'd just bought the joint. Silently we surveyed the empty room. 'No need to worry,' he said. 'The people will come.'

The dancer turned out to be his sister. He brought her in from Sheffield, paid her a couple of beers and dinner if she'd dance, liven up the place. She eased her way over and sat down on a milk carton.

'You're a terrific dancer,' I said. 'I saw you from the road.'

'Okay,' she said.

I ordered a dark rum. In spite of the hour, in spite of the amount I'd had to drink, I was feeling sober, a sure danger sign, and I made a mental note to myself not to drink too much more, not to drink myself 'out of the girl' so to speak. Flickering just at the side of my vision was a picture, perhaps a memory of myself, stumbling around a living room, blurry-eyed, thick-faced, muttering, 'Where's the bedroom? Where's the bedroom?' to my horrified date.

I congratulated myself on the prudent choice of dark rum over white rum. Lily's wallet sat on the counter and I was tempted to have a peek through it. But wasn't that how this binge started, the photo in J.'s kitchen, the happy family in the apple orchard? No, I said to myself, leave it alone. But it proved too tempting. It always proves too tempting. Years ago, in my early twenties, when I was very single, I loved waking up in a girl's apartment in the morning and going on a little snoop patrol after she'd gone to work.

I savoured that delicious moment when her alarm went off. To lie there in the early morning light, the sun shaded by yellow blinds and to listen, half awake, half asleep, to the sounds of a girl getting up: the drawers opening gently, the rustle of underclothes, the water rushing in the sink, the silhouette of a woman slipping a dress over her head, her movements getting firmer, more decisive as she wakes up. And then the moment of truth. Is she going to let you stay or make you leave with her? The hand on your shoulder, the same hand you remember from the night before, and she leans over and smells delicious in the morning, soap and clean hair, still damp from the shower. The kiss on your cheek and then the voice, smelling of lilacs. 'It's okay,' she whispers, 'go back to sleep.'

And then the rattle of keys, the door shutting, the sound of retreating footsteps and then falling back down, down into sleep in a bed that smells like her, in a room that smells like her.

When you wake up near noon, the sunlight is softer, the greens and yellows in the street more muted. And then you have a poke around her apartment, the address book, the cartoons and photographs and recipes and mementos stuck to the fridge with tiny magnets, the top left-hand drawer where she keeps jewellery. A look at the calendar: who is R. and why was she supposed to phone him last night? Why does she have five Nana Mouskouri albums? And then you're on your way. But first one more thing. It's always fun to phone a friend from a new woman's apartment. 'Guess where I am? Yes siree-bob! I'll see you at the Circus!'

Lovely really, those leisurely strolls over coffee through another person's life.

But Lily's wallet. It was grey, good leather, and when I opened it, it smelt like her. Credit cards, restaurant receipts, three business cards, a birth certificate. Born 1952. Thirty-three years old. A grown-up at least.

A photograph, old, cracked. I looked quickly at the toilet. The coast was clear. I held it up to the light: two pencil-thin teenagers standing on a beach somewhere. The girl is obviously Lily. She covers her eyes and looks self-consciously into the camera. The other person, I assume, is Jack, although the difference is stunning. This young man stands narrow waisted, almost cocky in the hips, smiling superciliously over the photographer's shoulder. A straw hat sits atop shoulder-length Molière-like hair. At the bottom of the picture, scratched in ink, is Formentara 1972.

Fourteen years ago. The year of the Kansas City girl. But Formentara. Something flutters in my stomach.

Formentara, a bleak sand-swept island a night's ride by ship from Barcelona. I went there with my best boyhood friend the summer of my first year in university. We built a ramshackle hut on the tip of the peninsula where we were surrounded on three sides by the sea and the wind and we sat out on the rocks, letting our hair grow wild, our skin turning the colour of dark mahogany. We had been there three weeks when one scorching day we were sprawled in the shade of our shack, panting like dogs from the heat, staring sun-glazed down the beach, when suddenly at the far end, miles away, a tiny stick-like figure appeared against the horizon. It wavered in the heat against the white sand and the blue sky. We watched it for a quarter of an hour. There was something familiar about this stick figure, its straight up-and-down carriage, its quick walk. My friend and I looked at each other wordlessly. Was it possible? Could she have tracked us down from London (where we'd left her packing plastic dinosaurs in the museum), through Paris, through Barcelona, all the way here, to this finger of sand pointing into the middle of the Mediterranean?

It's mid-July. A nineteen-year-old girl walks along the white sand of Formentara, sees two prostrate figures in the broiling sand, laughs, and her laughter carries to us; it's her signature, noisy and full of excitement and a little too loud because she's not sure she's welcome. Her hair comes into focus, straight and brown and parted in the middle and then her cheek bones high and chiselled and then her eyes squinting against the sun. J. closes the final twenty yards and drops her dunnage bag into the sand. 'Well,' she says, and there's that nervous shriek of laugher again. 'What do you say? Can I stay?'

I snapped the wallet shut. I looked about guiltily for Lily. Where was she? How long had she been gone? Twenty minutes? Impossible to say. For a second I thought she'd ducked out the back door. But no, her wallet, it was still here. I went around back of the bar and peered into the woman's washroom. No Lily. I looked under the toilet door. No feet. But when I came back to the bar, she was there, chatting easily to Bill. How could I have missed her? Didn't I have a little chat with myself about this, about the juice and how things get? Never mind. She's back.

'Say,' I said to Bill. 'Do you have "Night Nurse"? I've been trying to hear that song since I got here.'

'I think it's somewhere here,' he said uncertainly. 'But I haven't unpacked all my records.'

'How does it go?' Lily asked. 'Sing me a couple of bars.'

'No,' I said.

'You sing me a couple of bars, Bill.'

Bill hummed a few bars, in perfect pitch while his sister watched from the milk crate.

'I don't think I know it,' Lily said, as if she were taking a Beethoven quiz. 'No, I don't think I recognize that piece.'

There was something about her polite formality that suited her, that she wore with ease and made her very attractive. A kind of democratic world view where all questions were equally interesting, all mysteries equally perplexing and worthy of attention. But I wasn't going to sing 'Night Nurse' for her. I was on a roll, no question about it, but I'll never be hot enough to sing 'Night Nurse' in an empty discotheque to a woman I just met.

'Let's go to the Wharf Club,' I said. 'They'll have it there. They've got everything there. It's the best bar in the world. You're really going to love it.'

Bill flipped on his ear phones. His sister stood up as the music started and danced with her back to us, moving as if she were skiing in slow motion, those bare brown arms in their U.S.A. T-shirt.

The road turned down, followed a half-moon course, running along the sea, past the coffin makers where an oil lamp burned in the window and a black figure bent over in the shadows. Lily crossed the road and peered in the window. The figure turned around and she waved, a delicate little fan of a wave. He waved back and I could see the wood chips in his eyebrows and hair.

'That's not a coffin maker,' she said. 'That's a furniture shop.'

'I thought they made coffins there,' I said. 'Children's coffins.'

'Don't be morbid.'

I crossed over the road and knocked on a plate-glass window.

The carpenter looked up and opened the door. Lily trailed along behind me.

'What's up?' she asked.

I addressed the man in front of me. 'Do you have any coffins here?'

'Well,' he said, smilingly puzzled, 'I don't really know.'

'I'd appreciate it if you could find out.'

It was a huge shop, smelling of freshly sawed wood. At the far end, working under the classic naked light bulb, were two young men. In patois the man asked them earnestly if they had any coffins. I rather hoped they didn't. It had seemed like an amusing idea on the road but now under the glare of the light bulb the humour had quite melted away. The two young men disappeared into a room off to the side and we stood in the wood dust and silence. Soon there were creaks and the sound of a chair being overturned, before a black curly head popped into view, almost at a right angle to the floor, huffing out a sunrise-coloured coffin. Deep as an old-fashioned bathtub and smelling like a summer cottage, it was beautifully smooth and just looking at it made me comfortable and sleepy and I felt like cuddling up in there for a snooze.

The five of us stood expectantly around the coffin, everybody deadly serious, the three carpenters waiting for me to open the bidding. That was understandable: they'd stopped work, lugged out a 150-pound hunk of wood and now they wanted something for it. I knew I should do something but I couldn't think what. Buy them a drink? Good idea but the picture of us five tramping down to the Wharf Club was too absurd.

'Well, thank you, chaps,' I said crisply in my plantation owner's voice, and made to leave. But it wasn't going to be that simple, and they looked at me and then at each other, confused.

'How much is it?' I blurted out.

'Five thousand dollars,' one replied.

'Say,' I agreed, as one connoisseur to the other, 'that's a damned good price.'

We all nodded and contemplated the coffin. The scene might have gone on indefinitely if Lily hadn't intervened.

'We're just looking,' she said and reached decisively into her wallet, pulling out a blue Jamaican ten-dollar bill.

'Thank you for your trouble,' she said. The bill slipped from her fingers and fell onto the red, dust-covered floor.

'It's all right,' the son said, bending over to pick it up but Lily beat him to it.

'You don't tip enough,' she said to me, and for a second I could have sworn I was talking to J. Even the intonation was the same, the matter-of-fact tone indicating an unattractive, personal shortcoming.

'I've noticed all night long,' Lily continued. 'You never tip anybody.'

'Yes I do,' I said, looking to the three men for support. 'I'm on a tight budget.'

'You should always tip,' she concluded, 'no matter what the service is like.' The carpenter and I exchanged neutral glances.

'Do you think this is the best place to discuss it?' I stared gloomily into the coffin.

'It's the *only* place to discuss it,' she retorted and the old carpenter laughed. That surprised me. He just didn't seem like the kind of man to get a joke like that.

'I do so tip. I left a tip at Murphy's for the beer.'

'That's because they didn't have any change,' she said.

Maybe Jack was right about wanting to take Lily outside and throttle her.

'Let's go outside, Lily,' I said in a voice not my own.

The young man with the ten-dollar bill glanced over

at his partner and then, having reached a subliminal agreement, said, 'Four thousand dollars.' This was getting impossible. They must have assumed that the tipping quarrel was something Lily and I did in *all* the coffin shops around town, a consumer variation on good cop, bad cop.

'No, no,' Lily said, touching the hand with the money in it. 'We're not buying today.' We backed out into the street while the brothers slogged the wooden box into the back room and the old man clicked shut the door lock, gave us a gentle, other-worldly wave and went back to his lathe.

'It makes me furious,' Lily said. 'People who don't tip.'

A bicycle swooped by with a young man and woman on it. She sat on the crossbar with her legs over the handlebars, trying to keep her skirt down. Under the glare of a street lamp, a man like a black Napoleon sat stiff and still on a gleaming motorcycle. He wore a beret and a parachute suit and dreadlocks framed his face. His teeth were tobacco-stained and he looked very proud.

'Do you remember me?' he asked.

I looked at him and remembered his face from the first time I came to the island. He was a beach kid, wandering up and down the shore all day long. He had short hair then and long trousers and he'd spent half an hour trying to sell me a pair of bongos.

'Holmsy?'

'I haven't seen you for a long time, but I recognized you straight off.'

'You look prosperous, Holmsy. No more bongos?'

A soft, falsetto laugh. He tapped the side of his nose and sniffed.

'No money in bongos. What can I get you for the head?'

'A noose, Holmsy. A noose.'

'Cool nuh,' he said, 'Cool.'

We left him on his chariot, his hand stroking a whispy beard on the end of his chin.

Chapter Fourteen

Finally the quay came into view and we turned the last corner by the boarded-up fruit stand. Henry the madman cried for justice in the town square, hurled out warnings and oaths, his voice booming like a cannon shot far out at sea. In the daytime, kids threw stones at his feet as he danced up the road. At night, with a shoe tied to his belt, he called down the gods.

And suddenly there it was, the Wharf Club, a squat, dirty bar beside the sea. A cement bunker with a tin roof and no windows. The birds awoke in the jungle. A dog slept in the doorway and we stepped over him. The jukebox glowered blue and lazy in the corner covered by a thick mesh wire. Two Jamaicans moved in the shadows and a sad country tune lamented in the haze:

Put your head on my shoulder
Let your tears run down my cheeks.

A string of Christmas lights blinked over the bar, over photographs of Jack Kennedy and Marcus Garvey.

The place smelt of sweat and piss – stronger than I remembered. In the centre of the room there was a circular table with a three-faced carved head mounted on it. On the head sat a glass vase of dead flowers. In the back of the bar, where the gloom zipped you in like a blanket, there were the 'love cubicles.' These were three concrete pill boxes behind a stone screen. In each were a table and two chairs. They were like tiny rooms with eye holes cut in the stone. If you wanted a little privacy, you could go back there, you and your date, and have a quiet drink while watching the goings-on in the bar. Because of the impenetrable black, no one could see you. There was something childishly exciting about it and I'd always wanted to take a girl there. I had my eye on 'love cubicle' number one, but there was no hurry.

We went to the counter. The Jamaicans nodded. 'Okay,' they said. They checked out Lily and went back to talking. A couple of whores – one with a long, striking face and black jumpsuit – glided in off the street and settled around the jukebox. They asked me in patois if I had any dimes, asked me if I wanted any pussy; thanked me for the dimes and punched in a couple of lethargic tunes. They checked out Lily too.

The bartender was asleep with his head on the counter. I knocked my knuckles on the bar, lightly, as I'd seen the old man do.

178

'Nobody?' I said. It sounded inexplicably foolish.

One of the Jamaicans poked the bartender and he looked up.

'Where's Ben?' I asked him. Ben was a tall, hunch-backed bartender. He used to run the place, a pleasant, friendly guy. He used to make me feel like I lived there and in a place like the Wharf Club, I found that flatter-ing.

But this bartender, a surly kid in his early twenties, wouldn't play ball.

'Huh?' he said sourly.

'Where's Ben?'

'You mean Herbert. Only the tourists call him Ben.' Great. Round one and a bloody nose already.

'Where's Herbert?'

'Gone.'

'He used to run the place.'

'He don't no more.'

'Conway told me he was still here.'

'Conway's crazy. Soft.'

'Well who owns it then?'

'Mr. Jenkins,' he said deferentially. He pointed to a picture beside Kennedy and something sank in my stomach. Mr. Jenkins was a foul-mouthed pot-bellied hamster of a man. He talked in a shouting whisper. I'd seen him around the place before and couldn't imagine why they hadn't thrown him out or shot him.

'Mr. Jenkins owns half the town,' the boy said. 'Ben works at the gas station. He moved out last year. Couldn't make no money.'

'I thought it was a family business.'

He laughed sleepily. 'Everybody gettin' poor.'

There was a rumble of thunder in the hills and the ceiling felt very low. The bartender put on a pair of paramilitary reflector sunglasses.

Lily stood beside me, observing, sleepy-eyed.

'Can I have a drink?' In the dimness, my voice sounded too cheerful, too eager to please.

'You've got a drink' he said, indicating the half-drunk disco beer.

'What's your name?' I asked.

'What do you want to know my name for?' He looked at Lily. 'What to drink?'

'Let me have a depth charge. I'd feel a lot better if you took those sunglasses off.'

Lily shifted her weight from one foot to the other. I wanted it to go well but something wasn't clicking in.

'Clifford. My name is Clifford. Never heard of a depth charge. What that?'

Gratified by his curiosity, I went on. 'Ben made it for me. Herbert rather. It's a shot of scotch in a shot-glass. You drop the whole works into a glass of beer.'

'No, I never hear of it.'

'Well can I have one anyway?'

'We have no scotch, sir. We only sell scotch during the season. Otherwise it sit in the corner and nobody drink it.'

There was a plink of rain on the metal roof. Outside the doorway, where the street light was sucked in, I could see the drops falling. Lily sat down. The chair was wobbly and she balanced herself very still and looked around. I noticed, just fleetingly mind you, that she looked a lot like J., particularly from the right side in silhouette, and I wondered why I hadn't seen that before.

'Overproof,' I said to the bartender. If there's one thing you can be sure of, it's that if you drink overproof, at some point in the evening somebody is going to sink into a puddle of tears. It's like gravity.

'I'm roasting,' Lily said. 'Why did I wear this stupid sweater? It makes me look as if I don't have any tits.' Then very deliberately she gave me a 'meaningful' stare, cockeyed for sure, for now I don't think Lily could have read a street sign without covering one eye, but there was that special glint, the drunk at the party who figures he's 'got your number.' It says: 'You can't fool me, buster. I'm onto you.'

The bartender brought over a six-ounce bottle of overproof, a can of pineapple juice, a plastic bowl of ice and two glasses. He whacked the can with his ice pick and left. I poured two shots, topped it with pineapple juice, dropped in a cube and waited for the worst. Lily was silent but she was cooking about something.

'Are you on vacation or what?' she asked thickly.

'You mean did I take off three weeks and jeopardize a partnership?'

'It's just very rare for a father to take his daughter on vacation.'

She was repeating herself. She was drunker than I was. She sipped her overproof, wrinkled her nose in disgust and shivered.

'God,' she said and then apparently forgetting the thrust of her own question, rambled on. 'No, this little jaunt was for Jack's benefit. He wanted to lose some weight and stop drinking.'

I nodded sympathetically.

'It's the pressure that makes him drink, right?' she said dryly.

'That's right.'

'Well now that he's here, he has no responsibilities so he can get as bombed as he wants.'

She took another sip of the overproof and considered it.

'Almost,' she said, remembering something very distant which had zoomed into focus, 'like chemistry class, like we're just about to autopsy something dead.'

One of the whores we'd seen earlier on the church

wall walked through the door and quite shamelessly approached our table.

'I would like to braid your hair,' she said to me.

'That's better than wanting to suck my cock for twenty dollars,' I replied philosophically. The line sounded very funny to me, and I laughed out loud. But I was alone. The whore called me a queer in a loud voice and Lily frowned. I was relieved when she resumed her monologue.

With a touch of self-pity, she continued. 'It's not bliss watching your boyfriend get drunk every night.'

'I can imagine,' I said, the heartburn tearing up my chest like a surgeon's scalpel. But then she took a roller-coaster detour that caught me off guard: 'I really like him though,' she said. 'He's neat.' That jarred her memory. 'So are you here on vacation or something?' she repeated.

'No, I came down here to write a book.' Like the genie in the bottle, out it popped. I just opened my mouth and the words tumbled out. I looked in my glass. I don't know why I picked that moment to lie. I'm not by nature a liar. But that's the thing with a whopper: once you tell one, you have to tell another. And then another. And then you have to remember them all.

'Actually it's more of polish job. I got an advance from my publisher.'

She looked visibly impressed. We both did. Why, in a moment we'd be talking about my upcoming and tiresome trip to Oslo.

'So what's it about?' she asked dully.

'Well, in a nutshell' – an apt choice of words – 'it's about a guy who comes to the tropics and loses his marbles.' I trailed off and there was silence. This was great, the kind of device only a Catholic could dream up.

'Like what's his name's book,' she offered.

'Yeah, exactly.'

A long meditative silence from my friend as the black swirled around us.

'Good story,' she said levelly.

'You know, Lily,' I said, leaning forward, my face flushed, 'back there in the restaurant I really felt like I'd fallen in love with you.'

Suddenly the pair of us reminded me of a tipsy secretary and her gin-bloated boss getting loaded at the local Holiday Inn.

'Nonsense,' Lily retorted amicably. 'I don't know *what* you need.' And then with an uncharacteristically lecherous chuckle she added, 'but I could think of a couple of things you wouldn't mind having.'

We sat silent for a while longer.

'Does your daughter go to school?'

'Yes.'

She wanted to talk about Franny some more and she was getting obsessed about it. And there was, in her obsessiveness, even more J. than before. Put a half-dozen Heinekens in Franny's mother and she gets a bee in her bonnet immediately. She can badger the truth out of anyone. Whether, in my case, I'd been unfaithful to her that summer of 1972 in Kansas City or whether, more recently, I'd sucked on a tuinal just before the last production meeting at the film festival. (I can still see her squinting at me down the full length of the board table, searching for a telltale sign of sloppiness. Of course the straighter I tried to act the more I slurred my words and spilled my coffee.)

No, when J. got it into her bean that she wasn't getting the straight goods, she'd drive you out of the country before she'd let a lie stand. And come to think if it, Lily's approach was not unlike J.'s. Like a shark she made a couple of innocent passes.

'I'm just cruising the neighbourhood,' she seemed to say. 'There's no fuss. Enjoy your swim.' It was only *after* you got out of the water that you realized you were missing a leg.

Lily persisted. 'Do you think she's missing out on any activities at school?'

'I don't think bobbing for apples is something to put off a trip to Jamaica for.'

'I've hit a sore point,' she said.

'No, just a sensitive person.' Groan. The sentiment had seemed like a sparkling parry, but it came out sounding very weak indeed, an ungainly thrust with a rubber sword. 'I'm tired of being treated like a nincompoop,' I said, settling the matter once and for all.

With a small flick of her head she indicated the overproof still face down on the table. 'That stuff isn't helping either. You're drinking formaldehyde.'

'Yes, Lily, but I'm having a great time.'

That thick-witted glint again. God, did I travel fifteen hundred miles just to end up spending another evening with J.?

'There's something going on here,' she said. 'Your wife, your daughter, something very odd. And believe me I'm used to strange goings-on.'

'You're starting to annoy me again,' I said offhandedly. But there was no throwing this little choo-choo off its monorail.

Rather demurely she excused herself to return to the bathroom but when she got back trouble broke out again like a fresh rash. The tiff began over a principle, I guess, the way those tiffs always seem to. Naturally I can't remember which principle but I do know that we ended up quarrelling about – if you can believe it – Picasso. The silliness of the argument makes my palms sweat to this day but here's how it went. 'He knocks me out,' I said. I should have zipped it up right there but sometimes the speed and associations of my own brain impress me a great deal, particularly when I've been drinking and I fancied myself on the brink of a shimmering perception.

'Yes,' I said, quite transported, 'his Blue Period reminds me of Joyce's *Dubliners*.'

Lily snorted unbecomingly. 'Then it couldn't take much to knock *you* out,' she said.

It was a featherlight blow but these things, these mood swings, are touchy affairs, more a matter of context than logic, and I fell into a sulk and sucked back the rest of my stagnant pineapple juice. Worse, I had the uncanny impression of seeing my own teeth as if through the bottom of the glass and it was not an attractive vision.

'I'm going to ignore that remark but you know what I'm thinking,' I said darkly.

'Not the faintest,' she answered.

'You and Jack do this all the time.'

She looked very calmly at me and kept her gaze steady. Finally a thought flickered across her face and she dismissed it like a housefly. I'd got it wrong. They weren't like that. I started in about something else, trying to dispel the aura of unpleasantness. Lily appeared to listen. She was definitely hearing something but I don't know what. Finally I said, 'Lily, where *are* you?'

In a moment she answered. 'Anyone who compares

Joyce to Picasso is an asshole,' she stated quietly.

'Likewise.'

'Meaning what?' she said.

'Meaning fuck you.'

'Well fuck you too,' she said. 'Just fuck you too.'

Involuntarily I reached out my hand, perhaps to steady the table, maybe to grab her, but in any event I missed and she was gone.

The boys at the jukebox watched her leave with child-like amusement and looked at me sympathetically.

'You mash up,' one observed.

'She be back,' responded his friend. I wasn't so sure. The evening, as they say, seemed to be taking its own course.

Jauntily, as if I have women smash out of bars on me all the time, I bounded over to the jukebox and began, somewhat vocally I'm afraid, to search for 'Night Nurse.' And I found it. I looked around gleefully, stuffed my hands into my pockets after a couple of Jamaican dimes, and clicked them into the slot at the top of the jukebox. I pumped in the number JF.

'We are about to hear from Mr. Gregory Isaacs,' I announced hysterically to the bar.

Then the first mellifluous chords bounced into the bar and the liquor-smooth voice of Mr. Cool began:

Tell her just to get here quick
Woman attend to the sick

There must be something you can do
This heart is broken in two.

Sweet enough to break your heart. Already I missed
Lily. I wished she'd come back in here and we could
make up and listen to the song together. Around the
bar there were nods of approval. The whores swayed
in the gloom, even the sullen Clifford responded,
almost imperceptibly, his black sunglasses rising and
falling a millimeter in time with the music. And for that
one tiny second, the night, the trip, the horror of the
day before fell from my shoulders like a suffocating
cloak.

Crazy Henry whooped and hollered in the street. In
the bar the black men came and went. I watched them
swim around like exotic beautiful fish in an aquarium.
They wandered into the bar, men with names like Del-
roy, Churchill, Neville and Chicken, tall men in berets,
military hats, dreadlocks and gleaming wrist watches.
You could see them lined up on the bar, wrist after
wrist, impatient bored hands with beautiful, beautiful
watches. They floated in off the street and they floated
out again.

'*I don't want to see no doc,*' sang the honey voice, '*I
need attendance from my nurse around the clock....*'

God, I love it, I thought, I love it, I love it. I want to
stay here forever.

Chapter Fifteen

In the corner of my eye something hulky blocked the light, paused and came unsteadily in. It was the American Legionnaire from the plane. He was drunk and alone and he came up to the bar and looked over with red eyes. He was breathing in short puffs, as if in the middle of a bowel movement. An ugly mood, the anger pouring off him like sweat. Clifford picked up on it.

'All the fun people gone,' Red Eyes grunted. 'Just the scum left.' Clifford hesitated for a second. 'That's all right,' he said and slid him a beer with a very sharp, cold stare. It was a 'mind-yourself-sir' stare and it was effective. This was not Clifford's first stint on the graveyard shift.

'The whole town's shutting down,' Red Eyes said. 'Nowhere to eat.'

'We have food here,' Clifford responded automatically.

'You got to be kidding son.'

Clifford stood quietly. 'A serious man,' his silence said, 'says things only once.'

The Legionnaire looked over at me with a slow, bovine swing of his head. He came into focus on me. I felt a little flag flutter at the side of my throat and I knew it was a warning.

'What have you got to eat?'

'Chicken.'

'Chicken it is.' He moved away towards the back. You could feel the heat die down.

'Seems like a very nice guy,' I offered. Clifford shrugged. Wouldn't commit himself, wouldn't take my side. I needed an ally. I didn't know what the Legionnaire was doing back there but I could feel his eyes pressing into my back like two hot thumbs.

A shirtless Dread strode across the threshold of the bar. He nodded at Clifford then bent over with a high-pitched pink-gummed laugh. He asked Clifford why he was hiding behind those sunglasses. Said he looked like a 'tief' from Kingston. 'Why you squiggin' up, man? You frighten people.' They shook hands.

'Ah just cool off like dat, man.'

The Dread eyed me with relish, gave his leonine black mane a shake. He had a big tawny chest and he loved it. He struck it right in your face and I knew he was going to try to sell me something.

'Why don't you buy some land here?' he said to me. 'I can get a nice little piece by Lucea.'

I wasn't expecting that. A spliff maybe, a few pills,

some cocaine but not a mortgage with a lease / buy option. Not here, not at the Wharf Club at four o'clock in the morning.

'Maybe I should just give you the money and you'd come back with the land?' I said.

'Why not?' he laughed. 'See here now. Give me two dollars for a beer. My throat's very dry.'

'No.'

'A dollar for some cane.'

'No.'

He giggled again, this odd girl's laugh, and glided back into the night.

'Can I buy you a drink, Clifford?' I said.

He motioned to a chalk-scrawled sign over his shoulder: Staff is not allowed to accept strong drinks while on duty.

'How about a beer then?'

'I don't drink when I work.'

'But the sign says....'

'I don't care what the sign says.'

'Fine then.'

'You should have bought that man a beer, since you want to buy a man a drink,' he concluded.

This was a kick in the pants but it made me per-versely determined to win him over.

'Strong stuff this overproof.' I was taking a new tack. I was the endearing tourist, a good-natured, naive traveller who finds himself mickey-finned by the local brew. But it was too transparent. I'd fired back the first overproof too easily, with too much professional élan to pull it off. Besides I stank of the stuff.

'Sometime it knock you down,' he said.

'Right,' I said. 'You can drink it or drive your car with it. Say, is it true that when you drop a bottle of white rum on the floor, it explodes?'

Gracious we're tipsy and dear me you'll have to call me a cab. He wasn't buying that either but he was coming around. I could see that. I took a thoughtful sip. It sent a shudder through me. My stomach was giving me the yellow light.

The racy-looking whore wandered over to the Legionnaire; they exchanged hushed words and she sat down. A slow dance in her arms, a quiet smooch in love cubicle number three and who knows? He could turn into Franny's grandfather.

'I'm really getting plastered,' I said to Clifford. 'My wife is coming today.' The white rum was pushing me sideways. I explained, 'I'm not getting drunk because my wife is coming. I'm glad she's coming. I'm with my daughter. We're going to have a ... ' My voice trailed off and I felt something like warm water lapping at my toes; no need to be concerned, I thought, they're changing the water in the tank. Clifford sat down. I continued, 'They should have hammocks in here. They have hammocks at Pee Wee's. It's a very good set-up. You can lie down without going home. Besides,' I whispered, 'you don't have to get your feet wet.'

Clifford ignored the remark and I felt a stab of loneliness.

'How old is your little girl?' he asked.

'Five.'

'And she live with her mom?' Clifford joined.

'It's not an either / or situation.'

Clifford was chewing on a golf tee. With exaggerated precision he removed it from between his teeth and said, 'But she live with you?' I didn't know what he was getting at. The remark rankled me. I didn't want it to spoil anything. I wasn't going to let a casual presumption ruin my evening.

'I'm not meeting her mother till later. I'm going to get some sleep first,' I said.

'No more up and down for you,' he replied, grinning.

'I beg your pardon?'

'You can't go up and down the road at night with a kid,' he explained. 'You stay at home.'

Outside the rain fell more loudly. It was almost morning. I glimpsed a picture of Franny and me, watching the water fall in tropical sheets while no one spoke.

Out of the blue I felt a hand rest tentatively on my back.

'Gene.'

It was Lily and suddenly, flushed with excitement, I leaned over and impulsively kissed her.

'I want to go back there,' she said finally, and motioned towards the stony cubicles. 'There's something I've got to tell you.'

She touched my elbow with her hand and I moved away, to the back of the bar, past the lime-green toilet which swallowed abruptly as I passed, and into the booth. There was a little square table and two stools. It smelt bad back there because of the toilets. Through the stone grating I could still follow the activities in the bar.

Clifford, who had been on the cusp of becoming my best friend until thirty seconds ago, had returned his attention to a comic book which he appeared to be studying.

'I'm only telling you this,' Lily began, 'because I like you, because I find you simpatico.' I steadied myself for her confession of love. Perversely, even as I sat forward to bask in it, I felt my interest in her dwindling.

'I've had a terrible stomach ache for three days,' she blurted out. 'I'm terribly, terribly constipated. Do you know something I could take?' I don't know how long I looked at her, blank-faced, waiting for the words to rearrange themselves in an order which might make some earthly sense.

'I'm at my wit's end,' she pleaded.

I opened my mouth from habit to reply. The silence suggested it was my turn, but I was locked in neutral.

'I've tried akee fruit, bananas, hot beer....' As she neared the end of her list I could feel myself coming around.

'That's not supposed to happen in Jamaica,' was all I could manage.

Her eyes welled into tears.

'Do you think I've got cancer?'

'No, no,' I said quickly.

'Are you sure?'

'Positive.'

'Well what am I going to do?' she wailed. 'It's ruining everything.'

We lapsed into silence but tears, they're very contagious, and soon it was my turn. Just how I settled on the subject of my father's suicide I don't know, but like the debris from a depth-charged submarine eventually it too rose to the surface. It was an old-time crowd-pleaser but I'd kind of left it back with my university days. When it looked like Jesse Weston, Weltschmerz and thirty cups of coffee weren't going to get the girl, when I'd smoked so many cigarettes I had to gag between trips to the bathroom, when all this failed, I brought out the tragedy. Once I was double trumped. At the conclusion of my sad tale, the young woman, the daughter of a German paratrooper, unhesitatingly informed me that her father had shot her mother and then himself in front of the three horrified children. What could I say? She was my kind of gal and we lived together for three years.

Anyway back to the tragedy. I used to trot it out like that because, for many years, my father's death meant very little to me. It was such a furious and alien act that it seemed, to my young and very literary imagination, almost exciting. But then time went by, a lot of time, and one bright fall day, a day like a freshly minted penny, I finally understood, in my heart, that I was never, *ever* going to see him again and my stomach fell through the floor of the world and I stopped telling the story.

But for reasons I'm still fuzzy about, I picked Lily and the Wharf Club to go back into it. And while I began rather glibly, I didn't finish that way and at the end we were both pretty much shot-up, both in tears. Lily was because I was, and because the story and everything else in that moment seemed, like those moments do, very, very sad and she leaned over and kissed me on the mouth and said, 'I love you. I *really* do.' I moved closer to her and very softly nestled my face against her neck and touched my lips to her cheek. In the bar the beautiful fish swam around and around.

But then things moved on as they do and got pretty steamy back there in Love Cubicle Number One. It wasn't too long before we were rubbing up against each other like a couple of barncats.

'*What* are you doing?' she asked as she felt my hands leave her. 'God,' she said, 'I haven't spent the night in a bar with my hand in a man's pants for ages.' A lovely pause. 'This is *all* I can do, you know?'

We might have been in her dad's rec room, waiting for the car lights to flash against the garage door. With my forehead leaning against her bare shoulder I said: 'So how do you like the Wharf Club?'

'Beats killing my boyfriend,' she answered.

'Let me do something for you,' I said and I think I actually meant it.

'What happens,' she whispered, 'if Clifford comes back here to freshen our drinks?'

A cat slipped into the cubicle, settled itself on the floor and watched us. The Legionnaire slow-danced with the whore. I heard voices lull through delicious blue smoke. I felt the heat in the small of her back and smelt the fragrance of her neck. There was the sound of her hands under my shirt and my hands under her sweater. There were long, hot stretches of silence, the shriek of a bar stool grating on cement and then those funny, sudden flourishes of activity like the rapid making and unmaking of a bed.

'This is *it*,' she gasped, 'this is *all* I can do.'

Even before she said it, I felt it in her body and I knew what she was going to say.

'Jack's here,' she whispered. I looked out into the bar. I started at the left side and slowly swung my vision over like a camera. But there was no Jack. I looked up at the top of the stone partition in case there was a grinning gargoyle peeping down. No Jack.

'He's here,' she said urgently. 'He's close. I can feel him.'

A full thirty seconds later the doorway darkened with an apprehensive figure. It was Jack. He had the ghostly haunted look of someone who's just woken up in the middle of the night nauseated with jealousy. It had made him physically ill. And I understood exactly what had happened. J. always knew when I was unfaithful to her. She swore up and down she could tell, to the second, even from a thousand miles away, the moment my body touched another woman. Later she'd quiz me, get me drunk, hound me until I was too tired to deny it. And then, running on that quick, hysterical energy, she'd figure out the time and the place, even the time difference and mostly, like that time in Kansas City, she'd be right. I think the same thing happened to Jack that night. At some point along the road Lily said yes, and a mile away he woke instantly from a dead slumber.

Bolstering himself, Jack stepped into the bar and spoke to Clifford. It was unnerving how clearly we could hear his voice. With forced camaraderie he started into a story about eating boulla buns on the island's north shore when he was a kid. It was one of those pointless little anecdotes that come straight from the nerves. But the effect on Lily was immediate. I could feel her attention switch from me to him like a bright, yellow spotlight. It reminded me of trying to sustain a conversation with a mother when her slightly feverish child wanders into the bedroom. Her face hurt for him, for his confusion and for his blathering. She had more than forgiven him. Again.

She squeezed a piece of kleenex into my hand, slid out of the booth, passed quickly by the toilets and the glare of the jukebox and pushed up beside him at the bar. She said something to him, he replied with a question, she shook her head and put her arms around him and he closed his eyes in relief.

He looked over at the cubicle where I was watching them through the grating. He wanted to come over and, in some misguided, private-school way, he wanted to say something *big* to me, something to show me and the whole bar in fact that everything was all right, that *he* was all right.

But Lily would have none of it and I adored her in that moment. She caught him by the sleeve, said something firm to him. His resolve weakened, his face lost those phoney, nervous furrows and he followed her out.

Chapter Sixteen

What do you do when the night's over and you don't want to go home? Simple. Drink more.

I went back up to the bar in a mood which seemed, on the surface, loose-limbed and easy-going but which was in fact growing darker by the second. Somewhere in my passage across the bar, an invisible hand had shifted gears and I slipped from autonomous to anti-social. Every noise in the place, every loud laugh, every jostle from a shoulder distracted me, annoyed me as if I were being torn away from an absorbing project. I looked around at the the grimy walls, the dull plinking lights, smelt the piss from the urinals and I wondered how I could have played such a trick on myself. Why did I want to get back here so badly? Was it the hot sun on my back as I wound my way down the road? Was it the sea? What was all the fuss? I tried to imagine myself in Toronto imagining myself in Jamaica. I had a vivid recollection of waking up one morning with such a longing for Jamaica it made me dizzy. But what was it?

Yesterday when all this started I waited and waited to hear the sound of the plane's wheels skid down on the black tarmac in Montego Bay and then I waited to get to the hotel, to the white room. And then I was on the road and there was Dexter and Jack and Lily and the mud-coloured man with green eyes and then I wanted to close my eyes and wake up in the Wharf Club. The Wharf Club: it seemed in those fantastic hours to sit right dead in the centre of the world. But I'm here now and the place is a dive.

Years ago, when I first met Dexter, I used to come here in a black shirt and a panama hat and drink over-proof until the hallucinations came down. How tiresome that all seems now, these acts of self-extermination, the scorpion stinging itself to death, the tarantula devouring its mate, the scab-covered face looking back from the mirror in the morning.

I was in a sunny mood and I wanted to spread the sunshine around. But there was no one to talk to. The Legionnaire was settled in snugly with his whore. He was having fun. The idea that the Legionnaire was having more fun than me in my bar, it had a kind of droning inevitability.

A guy called Purple Face comes into the bar and I give him a sullen nod. He wants me to buy him a drink. He asks very friendly. Very smooth voiced. When they hustle you here, they take you by the wrist, like they're taking your pulse. I say no. He asks the bartender.

'Nothing till you pay,' Clifford tells him. 'You had two rums and didn't pay for neither.'

Purple Face looks bewildered. 'Not possible. Shame

on you,' he says. 'Chaw, chaw.' Purple Face says something to a wild-eyed man with a gold front tooth. Voices are raised. Clifford pulls out a three-foot horse cock – a mahogany club – and whacks it on the bar. It cracks like a gunshot. Everybody jumps. The argument is over. Clifford serves Purple Face a rum anyway. He makes a clicking sound with his tongue. 'Chaw,' he says and shoves it across. There's a reggae song on the jukebox. About drinking Heineken, smoking sensé and dancing with your girl. Pussy, booze and dope and Purple Face loves it. He puts a long black hand on his stomach and struts the length of the bar. Very smooth, very cool. He laughs and spits. It's four o'clock in the morning and the Legionnaire talks softly to the girl. Last chance for a slow dance.

Outside a car pulls up and guy in a red shirt gets out and comes into the bar. He's got a machine gun slung over his shoulder. The Legionnaire catches sight of the gun and jerks in his chair. It makes him real nervous, a coon running loose with a fine piece of lethal machinery. The whore giggles, touches his arm and he sits back, throwing up worried little glances.

Mr. Red Shirt works for the Eradication Squad, looking for the big marijuana fields in the hills. But when you see them in town this early in the morning, it means they're looking for a little action, some befuddled white guy to shake down for lunch money. Anyway we start talking, he and I. Turns out he's got a brother on the New Jersey police force. Two of his buddies come in – they've got machine guns too – and they drift off into patois. That leaves me and Purple Face. He's bugging me about a drink again and he's getting on my nerves. I say something to him, he says something back to me. I tell him to stuff it in his hat. That shocks him a bit and he asks me to repeat myself and I ignore him. At one point, when the rap from the gunners on my left gets going pretty fast and there's lots of guffawing and 'rasta-clots,' one of them steps to the door of the bar, yanks back the clip on his gun and blasts off a round into the night air. You can smell the gunpowder waft back into the room. The Legionnaire freezes like a man with a rattlesnake on his chest.

'Don't be afraid,' they say to him, and then there's more high-pitched guffaws.

Somebody puts a song on the jukebox and I feel as if I'm floating in a bathtub of dirty water, rocking like a metronome. I fancy a gin and tonic – I need a straight, clean hit, with good purchase – I order it from Clifford. At that moment, I figure I'll finish my drink and maybe even call J. from across the road. Thinking about the phone call makes me a bit edgy and when Purple Face starts nagging away at me again, this time to buy some sensé, I figure calmly, very cold bloodedly, I'm going to hit him. I'm going to wait until he puts down his glass and then I'm going to drop him. But then I remember Clifford and the horse cock and I think: No, do it outside.

'Purple Face,' I say, almost affectionately, 'put your drink down. I'm going to knock your block off.'

He takes a while to answer.

'I mash you up,' he says, looking straight ahead, 'when I finish my drink.'

So we go back to the drinks, in silence, side by side, as if we're in stalls at the raceway, each pretending not to notice what the other is doing.

Ages go by and my mood starts to mellow. I sort of feel like making up but my pal here is taking it hard. He's started shooting his mouth off, in patois, how I threatened him and what he's going to do to my bumbaclot ass when we get outside. The gunners say something back, real fast. I can't make out what it is. I'm hoping they're going to take my side, but from the sound of things they're not. They're not taking anyone's side.

'When I finish my drink,' Purple Face says to me, clicks his tongue and since the guys don't stop him, I figure they must be on his side. Anyway fuck it, I think, I could slam my hand in a drawer right now and it wouldn't bother me a bit.

I shoot a quick glance over at him. He's brawnier than I thought, a body like a bloody fisherman. Paddling after those barracudas all morning doesn't give a guy too thick a waistline. But anyway, I think, fishermen don't go to bars at five in the morning. Or do they?

I catch a glimpse of myself in the rust-spotted mirror. To be frank, I'm not looking too 'street' tonight. Particularly from the side.

Purple Face tells me to pass him the water. I do. It makes me feel better. He's stalling for time, watering down his rum. He fills his glass half way. That gives me twenty minutes. But then he surprises me. He drains the glass in a gulp, puts it down, says 'okay' and starts out the door. He stops at the doorway, makes a joke with the gunners, and they all laugh and *that* terrifies me.

There's that twitching again, right at the side of my throat and this is it. He's waiting. Everybody's waiting. I feel my body go into motion before I've even told it to. I'm following him out the door and I can't even stop myself. I feel sick to my stomach and I put out my hand at the doorway to steady myself. I'm going to throw up and then I'm dizzy and I feel like grabbing on to the doorway but then I have the picture of him pulling me into the street with my hand clinging to the side of the door and everyone howling with laughter, and then before I've told it to my hand lets go and I'm out in the street with him, face to face, under the spotlight, my temples flapping in and out like a bellows.

Das grosse Muffensausen.

'Okay, man,' he says, 'let's go.'

'Not here,' I say. 'Up that lane.' I point to the dark, dusty road leading up past the Wharf Club into

Reground. I'm thinking if I'm going to take a beating I'm not going to take it in front of the Wharf Club, not in front of the gunners or the Legionnaire and his whore.

Purple Face won't go for it. 'No man,' he says. 'Right here.'

'No,' I insist. 'Up the lane.' His mouth parts slightly in confusion. He looks indecisively up the black lane. He thinks for a minute. The gunners are milling around the door. They could be watching a couple of dogs fuck in the street.

'You're crazy,' Purple Face says. He's got a very deep voice. Sensing a glimmer of a way out, I jump at it like a man leaping from the third-floor window of a burning house. 'I'll show you how crazy I am,' I say, and I throw myself down on the ground in front of him, right on my back, and start kicking my legs in the air. 'This is how crazy I am,' I scream. At the far end of the street a car comes crashing around the corner, its lights bounding up and down and heading straight for me. The Red Shirt comes flying out of the bar and I feel a pair of rough hands grab me under the arms and yank me off the road, shoving me up against the side of a garbage can. It's not chivalry. You just can't have a white guy getting run over by a car on the main street in Paradise. It's bad for business.

The gunner leans over me. I can smell the rum on his breath. He's overheard our conversation. 'The next time you go up a dark alley with a Jamaican,' he says, 'he'll stick a knife in you.'

They all go back inside. I'm left there in the dust and the empty Red Stripe containers and the stench of the garbage. Purple Face is the last to go back in. Clifford is standing at the door. I look up at him and smile, a smile like the slit in an overripe watermelon. No acknowledgement. I hum a little ditty, something he can hear. It's the opening two bars of 'Night Nurse.' I get up, dust myself off and try to go back into the bar but when I try to squeeze past Clifford he gives me a hard shove in the ribs which sends me crashing back into the garbage cans. I prop myself up on my elbows. Well, I've finally done it, I think, I've finally gotten kicked out of the worst bar in the world. Maybe Lily is right. Maybe I don't tip enough.

On the horizon there is the very first smudge of daylight, like something behind a tattered curtain. The madman no longer cries in the street. A sheet of lightning flashes in the upper cloud banks. Bullfrogs twitter. A motorcycle passes, then a car. A man on a bicycle drags a dying snake through the deserted centre of town. On the quai a group of blacks yell 'Night Walker, Night Walker.'

A man in blue trunks leaps ashore with a wriggling octopus on his fist. 'A sea puss,' they cry like excited children. 'A sea puss, a sea puss.' The crowd gathers round. 'Kill it man, kill it!'

I step around the corner of the bar. A cyclist passes me with a warm good morning. The clouds hang low and grey like water blisters. The sun must be right over J.'s house by now. Cool and white it hangs in the morning chill. The road spirals unsteadily before me, reaching up into the hills where Franny is asleep, where Lily is asleep, where Jack is asleep. There's a hollow boom of dynamite in the mountains. A fisherman in dirty dungarees stands by the road. He asks me for a cigarette. I pass Wilson's fruit stand. He's up sitting in a rocking chair. 'What elixir for you? Mangoes, bananas, herb root? Make you like this all night.' He raises his forearm and smiles obscenely. 'Your wife no sleep tonight, I promise.'

He waves his fingers goodbye. And smiles. The tide is in. The waves splash disconsolately against the rocks. There is trash floating in the water, milk cartons, plastic cups. It's a sewer of a day when the whole world is hung over. The sea pulls back its lips to expose rotting gums and blackened stumps of teeth. I walk faster, up onto the seawall, past Tiger's café, empty now, potted ferns twisted and broken.

I step onto the seawall, with dread lapping at my ankles. If you're sick, go to the hospital. I walk along the wall, one foot in front of the other, tic, tac, don't step on a crack, faster now, left, right, left, right. In the back of a pickup truck a sea turtle awaits execution with a rope around its neck; up around the corner, past the church, shutters closed, bottle-green stained-glass windows, peeling paint, hedges overgrown, garden overgrown, plantain trees straggle across the unkempt lawns, past the coffin shop. 'Morbid. Don't be morbid.'

Past the gleaming motor-home police station: four perfect officers read the *Gleaner* and wait for something to happen, something other than cousin Franklin gone hacked up his woman with a machete. And there a hundred yards from me, a young girl with black hair walks freely and easily in the centre of the road. She crosses an empty field, past the Lone Star café. Behind her, unknown to her, a man in a sleeveless white sweatshirt walks quickly on short legs, trying to catch up. Dexter doesn't call out but quickens his pace after her. That'll be the night you open your door and wish you'd never been born. And then a sharp nauseating wave of panic. The divining rod hangs suspended then plunges straight down, frozen. Franny. How could I have left her unprotected in her bed? What if she woke up? Found herself alone? No father. No mother. No father. It must be near six-thirty. She'd awaken any second now. And what if something happened to her? What if someone got into her room? What if she walked in her sleep and fell down the concrete steps?

The black cars inch up the hill and a tent flap snaps in the lifeless wind. And then I was running up the road, temples pounding, what if, what if, what if, stale ditties of music popping into my head, what if something were to happen to her? What will we do without our baby? J., J., what will become of us? The evening spreading out behind me like garbage streaming from a speeding truck. I am the child's worst enemy. I run past Uriah's, past Pamela's. Uriah shouts my name. I keep running, the final stretch of road, John Crow circles overhead, the sea grey and quiet, the birds expectant, hushed, up the last hundred yards, stumbling in a pothole, twist my ankle, yelp in pain, stumble up the walkway, dash through the lobby and across the patio, sprint across the alcove, hear a crash and a tinkle of glass, and a child's startled cry. Up the steps, three at a time, rip open the door.... 'That's the night you'll open your door, open your door.'

In the patch of light in the doorway, a splash of blood, like a child's bloody fingerprints, another splash spreading into the shadow. My god, my god, my god. I rip the door open wider and the light spreads across the room, the blood leading to her bed, Franny sitting bolt upright, her features white and frozen, her eyes fixed on something behind my back. From the shadows beside her bed I hear a gurgle and then a blood-choked cough. Like a person coughing. A bird crashes on the floor in a mess of blood and shattered glass, its head impaled on a shard of glass in the window frame. Blood squirts from the clump of feathers in a thin stream, like ink from a fountain pen. A headless bird flops in a slow, spasmodic circle. A wing pushes the body forward, the breast black and shiny, and there are pools of blood like poppies and ghastly smears on the wall and Franny covered in glass. Seeing it's me, she hurls herself forward on the bed and throws out her arms. 'Don't leave me!' she shrieks. 'Don't leave me!'

Chapter Seventeen

It took the bird a long time to die. I didn't have the stomach to pick him up. I tried to nudge him out of the room with my foot but it was all too ghastly. There seemed nothing left to do but sit on the bed with Franny bawling on my lap and watch the blood-matted feathers rise and fall more and more unsteadily until, with one final flap, a flap that raised him six inches and turned him over, he landed with a wet thud and that was the end.

There was some hammering out in the yard. It was Conway pounding down a load of fresh stones around the mango tree. He put down his shovel and came up the cement stairs, none too quickly, and looked in the room. 'Stupid birds,' he said and wandered off into the back of the hotel for a broom, a bucket and a mop.

It's a funny thing the fascination children have with death. It was agony for Franny to watch the bird die, but once it was dead, when there was just the two of us again in the room, she couldn't take her eyes off the bird. She tiptoed around, crunching the broken glass under her sandals, peering at the battered feathers, then at me. She watched the whole thing, holding my hand to be sure, as Conway swept up the glass, heaved the bird into the bushes, washed down the blood stains off the floor and wall. She didn't want to leave the room until it was done.

For me, horror gave way to a terrible fatigue. I could hardly keep my eyes open. But there was something more than that. I felt flat and dead. Sometimes, in the course of that evening, there had been moments when I'd forgotten all about Franny, when even *that* part of me ceased to protect her. It felt as if I'd spent my life stealing out of white rooms to walk down dark roads – and every time I'm convinced that some night I'm going to stumble across something, a happiness as big as the sun. But it's a lie of course. There's nothing out there. When I lie in bed, I can hear my thoughts speeding up and suddenly I'm wide awake and ready. Even as I'm putting on my shoes I know it's a lie. And as I'm looking for my keys, I know it's a lie. But I go out anyway. I can't bear not to. Because if I try to go back to bed and turn out the light, it feels like the whole tide of life might just pick that very second to crash by my door and if I don't get out there, now, I'm going to miss it.

And it always ends up in the same place, a deserted town square at sunrise when even the madmen have called it a night. When I imagine a lovely future, which

I do all the time, I imagine the night that I wake up at three-thirty and I hear a woman's voice beside me and she asks what's wrong. And I say, 'Nothing.' That'd be great, to lie there in the dark, to feel yourself floating in warm currents like the South Seas pictures I saw when I was a kid, to think, for one fractured second, about the world rushing past the door, the white, excited faces, the shards of conversation, to imagine this beautiful stream of shattered glass flowing by under the moon, and to do nothing at all, to lie back and say fuck it and slip back down into sleep.

There comes a time when you've got to stop ducking and take a punch and Tuesday morning, that's when I took mine.

First of all, Franny and I had a little chat. Overdue maybe but very simple. I said I'd made a mistake, that we were going home. I anticipated a flood of questions but she surprised me. She only asked what she needed to know: when she was going to see her mother. I said today and that was the end of it. She was delighted; a little light went off in her face, a bubble of enthusiasm floated up through her body and she was suddenly very excited and wanted to do everything. I wanted to do some of the things I'd promised her.

But first we went down the road and telephoned her mother from the Yacht Club. I was very tired;

my head was buzzing; my vision seemed crystalline, too bright and I didn't pay much attention to the call. The details have remained a blur.

Franny spoke to her mother; J. got back on the line to me. I think I slurred my words because she asked me if I was drunk. I said no but it didn't matter anyway.

We agreed that she should fly here, today, and pick up the child. I was willing to bring her back but no, she didn't want that and I said fine. There was no remonstrance, for which I was thankful but slightly indifferent. We'd meet, that afternoon, at the Mo-Bay airport.

I was numb when I put down the phone. The clouds broke around ten that morning, just as we were climbing into the back of a taxi. We whirred down the road – the one I'd spent the whole night on – in what seemed like seconds flat. I never knew it was so short. I caught a glimpse of Otto. He had fat, white legs and wore a towel around his neck. He was walking up the road slowly, a beer in one hand and I confess I felt a bit envious at his self-reliance, his easy-going stride. The beach was almost deserted but Franny made a friend right off, a little black girl. Her parents were vacationing from Chicago and while the children splashed breathlessly in the water, running up and down the shore like sand-pipers, we talked about sunscreens and vitamin E.

The children swam till their lips turned blue, and

reluctantly they said goodbye. Franny and I stopped in town, at that yellow shop beside the bank, and bought a Bob Marley T-shirt for Franny and a 'Jamaica NO PROBLEM' T-shirt for her mother. Around noon a blue van stopped in front of the hotel and tooted its horn twice. Franny and I were ready, on the front steps with Conway. He held the door open for us, slammed it shut and shook my hand through the open window. 'Goodbye, little girl,' he said to Franny and tapped on the van roof and we pulled away. They don't play music when you leave. The vans are always quiet and ours was empty. The driver brought along his girlfriend for company. She wore bright green curlers in her hair. Going back to Montego Bay was like being wound in on the end of a line.

We stopped in Savanna-la-Mar to look for more passengers. It was a little fishing village by the sea. We sat in the sweltering heat and dust in the market and waited. The fishing boats had just come in and there was a great deal of excitement. There was no off-season in Savanna-la-Mar. Life just went on and on. We cruised up and down the main street, the driver shouting our destination out the window.

It was in front of a seaside restaurant that I saw Lily and Jack. They were having lunch and the street teamed around them and they seemed very much together. He talked; she laughed. She held her hands close together and I could see she was happy. We didn't stop; we just slowed down and the driver yelled out 'Montego Bay, Montego Bay,' and neither seemed to notice. The swimming had made Franny ravenous and unwisely I asked the driver to pull over. I went to one of those sidewalk fry shops and bought a couple of pieces of chicken and two bottles of ice-cold orange pop. I wasn't hungry but I was dying to put something in my mouth. Franny wolfed down her chicken, which surprised me. She's timid about eating strange food. I should have seen disaster coming but I was relieved she was eating.

We started off again, into the heat and up a narrow, winding road. The driver wanted to get the trip over quickly and he wasted no time. It wasn't too long before Franny's little face went ashen and she said to me with utter despair, 'I don't feel so good.' She was sick into my shirt which I got off in the nick of time. It was over very quickly, just one good shot and she lost the whole lunch, chicken, pop, and coco bread I'd forgotten she ate at the beach. There wasn't much to be done. The shirt was a mess and I threw it out the window. Franny perked up instantly, got the colour back in her face and said, rather sweetly, 'If ever I'm sick, I'd only let you or J. touch me.' We looked out the window. I thought about Dexter throwing his shirt into the bushes; it seemed like ages ago. But it made me laugh. Dexter Alexander. Was he asleep yet? Was he lying on his bed, scheming? And when he finally fell asleep, what did he dream about? What were the things that made Dexter Alexander's heart leap? The child chattered away happily and finally I had to feign sleep to escape her indefatigable curiosity. I closed my eyes but she was staring at me. 'I guess I'll never find out how it works,' she said with a theatrical sigh. How what works? Storm windows? Birds in the night? Life? But I'm hooked and the conversation carries on. We're getting warm and the child knows it. And then it's two o'clock and we're looking down on the Montego Bay runway, hazy in the sunlight, Franny all dressed up in an ice-cream white dress, very excited. We stand on the second-floor platform and there she is, across the runway, first out of the plane. Tall, pale, wearing a green sweatshirt. She carries a grey raincoat over her arm. Features tight, skeletal. She wears large, clear glasses but still she squints. Lights a cigarette before she steps off the rampart. Looks across the tarmac. J. can't see us behind the green-tinted glass. But Franny sees her. Lets out a delirious squeal. Behind J. a stream of coloured cloth pushes itself through the door like a bandana. Snowball, another load for paradise.

   J. walks briskly across the hot pavement, then pushes her way along the walkway into the roller rink and lines up first at customs, passport and declarations ready in hand. Franny darts from my hand, scurries down the stairs into the reception and is almost in her mother's arms before J. catches sight of her. I stand at the end of the room, too tired to do or say the things I planned to.

We must have looked like war veterans, J. and I. Like those yellowing warped photographs in the attic. And the all the holiday bustle, all that cheerfulness around. Could we ever have been nineteen? Fresh-faced, clear-eyed? It's been a long way since that noisy, willowy-limbed girl in my Shakespeare class, the girl who laughed too loudly, was terrified of the dentist and blew her tuition. Her hair was longer then, dark and straight and she hated it. 'Perhaps I'll have it all cut off,' she said one April morning a thousand years ago. In those days I saved the romance for the wan blood-less creatures with the high cheekbones and sullen faces, pin-up girls straight from the pages of *Death in Venice*. Girls who smoked thin cigars and read Baude-laire, lived in messy apartments and couldn't do any-thing. 'But Gene,' J. reminded me gently years later, 'There *weren't* any girls in *Death in Venice*.

She married me in the War Amputees Building. We should have got our divorce there. She punctuated her journal with the daily entry. 'Today is the most unhappy day of my life. I'm completely miserable.' But as she told me recently, 'No grief, no matter how shal-low, lasts forever.' J. with the undone Chaucer essay, J with the undone shirt in the hallway of Chinatown, J. who said: 'There are some things that you forgive at twenty that you don't at thirty.'

The list spins lazily on. A friend of mine told me a story once about anacondas. He said they mate only once and then they roll off into the jungle, sometimes without seeing each other for years. But when they meet again they raise their bodies high up from the jungle floor and wrap themselves around each other, swaying back and forth in the moist shadows. It's a lovely image and it gives me a lump in my throat because I always think about J. and me when I think about that story, but I don't think it's going to work that way for us. No, it occurs to me now – and I don't know why it's taken so many years – that maybe you can miss somebody without wanting them back, that maybe J. and I have already had our last dance under the eucalyptus tree.

Finally J. eases her way across the airport floor, through the suitcases and golf carts and overheated people. She looks brittle and furious. Perhaps I have forgotten to smile.

'How are you?' she asks.

'Fine. A little tired.'

She looks at my arm. 'How've you been?'

I can't think of an answer. A woman with a camera bustles over and snaps our picture, Franny in her mother's arms, me about to light a cigarette. A threesome. I miss them both already. In an hour they'll be on a plane and I'll be back here on this scalding promontory – ready for a vacation. Golf? Backgammon

after sunset, a cool midnight dip in a blue-lit pool ...
empty, all of it, without them. Like waking up in
paradise with a bit in your mouth. But if you wanted
warm slippers and a hot toddy before bed, maybe you
should have laid off the cocktail waitresses.

Still it's difficult to imagine life before her. I can't
remember what I looked like, walked like, sounded
like. Did I wear grey-flannel shorts and an airplane
propeller on my head? It's as if we worked on
Stonehenge together.

Edited for the Press by David Young
Design by Gordon Robertson
Cover drawing by Rosalind Goss
Typeset in Sabon and printed in Canada

For a list of other books
write for our catalogue
or call us at 979-2217

THE COACH HOUSE PRESS
401 (rear) Huron Street
Toronto, Canada M5S 2G5